S0-APN-255

Ulysses S. Grant

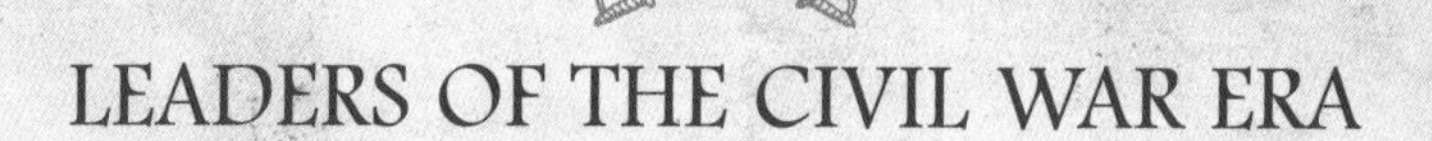

LEADERS OF THE CIVIL WAR ERA

John Brown

Jefferson Davis

Frederick Douglass

Ulysses S. Grant

Stonewall Jackson

Robert E. Lee

Abraham Lincoln

William Tecumseh Sherman

Harriet Beecher Stowe

Harriet Tubman

LEADERS OF THE CIVIL WAR ERA

Ulysses S. Grant

Samuel Willard Crompton

ULYSSES S. GRANT

Chelsea House
An imprint of Infobase Publishing
132 West 31st Street
New York NY 10001

Library of Congress Cataloging-in-Publication Data
Crompton, Samuel Willard.
Ulysses S. Grant / by Samuel Willard Crompton.
p. cm. — (Leaders of the Civil War era)
Includes bibliographical references and index.
ISBN 978-1-60413-301-1 (hardcover)
1. Grant, Ulysses S. (Ulysses Simpson), 1822–1885—Juvenile literature. 2. Presidents—United States—Biography—Juvenile literature. 3. Generals—United States—Biography--Juvenile literature. 4. United States. Army—Biography—Juvenile literature. I. Title. II. Series.

E672.C93 2009
973.8'2092—dc22
[B] 2008044613

Chelsea House books are available at special discounts when purchased in bulk quantities for businesses, associations, institutions, or sales promotions. Please call our Special Sales Department in New York at (212) 967-8800 or (800) 322-8755.

You can find Chelsea House on the World Wide Web at http://www.chelseahouse.com

Series design by Erik Lindstrom
Cover design by Keith Trego

Printed in the United States of America

Bang FOF 10 9 8 7 6 5 4 3 2 1

This book is printed on acid-free paper.

CONTENTS

1 The Ninth of April

It was springtime in Virginia. Red and brown soil was thick with mud as the last vestiges of winter disappeared. It was Palm Sunday, the ninth of April in the year 1865.

THE PLACE

Appomattox Court House was located in a small town and postal village along the river of the same name. About 60 miles west of Richmond, Appomattox, the capital of the Confederate States of America, had, until now, been spared the ruin and desolation that accompanied the Civil War—or, as many then called it, the War Between the States.

On the seventh and eighth of April 1865, the ruined remnants of the Army of Northern Virginia were encamped in and around Appomattox. The once-mighty Confederate army had been reduced to about 25,000 men, most of whom were in low spirits. Recently they had broken out from the nine-month-long siege of Richmond and Petersburg, only to be pursued across the southern Virginia countryside by the Army of the Potomac.

THE GENERALS

On the afternoon of Friday, April 7, General Robert E. Lee sent a letter to General Ulysses S. Grant. The leader of the Army of Northern Virginia asked the general-in-chief of all the Union armies (a title that was unprecedented in American history) what terms he might expect. General Grant wrote back to say that he was anxious to prevent the further spilling of American blood—whether Yankee or Confederate—and that he would insist on only one particular: that the men who yielded would be disqualified from serving against the Union again in this war.

Surprised by the relative leniency of his opponent's demands (Grant had become known as "Unconditional Surrender" Grant during the war), General Lee asked to meet in person. The request was granted and the two men rode, on the afternoon of Sunday, April 9, to Appomattox Court House.

THE MEETING

Twenty years later, in his book, *Personal Memoirs of Ulysses S. Grant*, General Grant recalled the moment when he entered the home of Wilmer McLean and beheld his Confederate opponent:

> General Lee was dressed in a full uniform which was entirely new, and was wearing a sword of considerable value, very likely the sword which had been presented by the State of Virginia; at all events, it was an entirely different sword from the one that would ordinarily be worn in the field. In my rough traveling suit, the uniform of a private with the straps of a lieutenant-general, I must have contrasted very strangely

> with a man so handsomely dressed, six feet high and of faultless form.

The contrast was marked. Born into the Virginia tobacco aristocracy, Robert E. Lee had graduated from West Point in 1829 without earning a single demerit, while Ulysses S. Grant had graduated in 1843, accumulating a considerable list of demerits in the process. Ever a meticulous dresser and always conscious of the symbolic importance of an occasion, Lee turned out in his Sunday best for this meeting on Palm Sunday.

Born into a family that had struggled economically for two generations and that lamented the loss of their former prosperity, Grant was what he seemed: a rough and disheveled man of the Old Northwest (which encompassed Ohio, Indiana, Illinois, and Michigan). Though Congress had raised him to the highest military rank of any American since George Washington, Grant had little time and less interest in manners or dress. He often wore shabby clothing, and he smoked cigars incessantly. Anyone meeting him for the first time would have difficulty recognizing the brilliant victor of half a dozen battles. Only upon engaging him in conversation would one learn that he was a man of great depth.

Grant and Lee had known each other in the Mexican War, and it was Grant who started the conversation, making small talk about earlier times. Before long, Lee brought to Grant's attention the reason for their meeting: He wished to surrender the officers and men of the Army of Northern Virginia.

Grant and Lee had fought each other for the past 12 months, with Grant pressing every advantage and Lee never yielding an inch. The embattled Confederates had fought bravely and well, but their sacrifices made no difference in the end. The vastly superior numbers and military equipment of the Northern armies had ground the Southern ones down. Both men knew this truth and both wished to keep the surrender from turning into a humiliation.

On April 4, 1865, General Robert E. Lee met with Lieutenant General Ulysses S. Grant at Appomattox Court House to surrender the Confederate Army of Northern Virginia. After four years of civil war, North and South had suffered greatly, with about 612,000 deaths and over a million casualties.

After some deliberate conversation, Grant called for paper and pens. Sitting there in the home of Wilmer McLean, Grant wrote out the following:

> I propose to receive the surrender of the Army of N. Va. on the following terms, to wit: Rolls of all the officers and men to be made in duplicate. One copy to be given to an officer designated by me, the other to be retained by such officer or

> officers as you may designate. The officers to give their individual paroles not to take up arms against the Government of the United States until properly exchanged, and each company or regimental commander sign a like parole for the men of their commands.

In the short capitulation agreement, Grant also wrote that Confederate officers were allowed to retain their sidearms (pistols) and personal baggage. Most importantly, he wrote that officers and men could return to their homes where they were "not to be disturbed by United States authority" as long as they observed their paroles. This was a remarkably lenient agreement from a man who, three years earlier, had responded to another request for terms with the simple answer, "No terms except an unconditional and immediate surrender can be accepted."

Grateful, quiet, and subdued, General Lee went to a side table to review the written terms. A number of popular artists sought to capture the moment, with Lee signing the surrender agreement, his closest military aide standing by the fireplace, Grant seated at the main table, and Grant's officers standing by the door. Every generation of Americans seeks to remember and recapture the amazing moment, at about 4:00 P.M., when Lee signed the document, thereby ending the long battles between the Army of the Potomac and the Army of Northern Virginia. Other battles still remained to be fought, and the Civil War would not entirely end until the summer of 1865, but the most important moment came in that two-story house at Appomattox Court House.

Grant did not ask for Lee's sword—there was no need. The two men walked out the door, with Lee headed back to the safety of his own lines.

Legend has it that the two men never saw each other again, but on the next day, Monday, the tenth of April, Grant rode out to the Confederate lines. Expressing a desire to see Lee once more, Grant was admitted to the Southern camp, where he and

Lee sat on horseback and spoke for half an hour. Lee remarked that the South was a big country, and it would take time for the Union forces to subdue it; Grant replied by asking Lee to use his influence to persuade his countrymen in other parts to yield. Lee felt that would be too much, that it would overstep his bounds as commander of just one army. Grant later recalled a pleasant interlude from that day:

> When Lee and I separated [for the last time] he went back to his lines and I returned to the house of Mr. McLean. Here the officers of both armies came in great numbers, and seemed to enjoy the meeting as much as though they had been friends separated for a long time while fighting battles under the same flag. For the time being it looked very much as if all thought of the war had escaped their minds.

The surrender ceremony of Palm Sunday had worked its magic. North and South, it seemed, could be reunited.

Ohio Boyhood

America's eighteenth president was not born in a log cabin, but the frame house was only one step up from it. Much is made of the Indiana boyhood of Abraham Lincoln, complete with rail-splitting and reading by candlelight; one often forgets that Grant's Ohio boyhood was made of the same stern material that shaped his great contemporary.

GRANTS AND SIMPSONS

Hiram Ulysses Grant (more on the name change later) was born at Point Pleasant, Ohio, on April 27, 1822. His father gave his first name; his middle name came from a relative on his mother's side who had recently read a novel about Ulysses (or Odysseus), the great hero of the Trojan War.

Jesse Root Grant and Hannah Simpson married in 1821 and moved to Point Pleasant, within sight of the Ohio River, where they started their family. Hiram Ulysses (whom everyone called Ulyss) was the eldest, followed by two brothers and two sisters.

Jesse was a hard man. Some photographs and likenesses display an engaging smile, but the man was primarily motivated by fear and ambition. His paternal ancestors, the Grants of Massachusetts and then Connecticut, had been prosperous farmers and merchants, but Jesse's family had gotten into financial trouble in his father's time. Raised with a painful consciousness of what it was like to come down in the world financially, Jesse wanted, more than anything else, to rise to prosperity and thereby to vindicate the success of earlier Grants. By the time his son Ulysses was born, Jesse was a tanner, taking animals' hides and boiling them, using chemicals to turn out leather goods. This was demanding work, and it turned him into a forceful, demanding man.

Hannah, Ulysses's mother, was gentler, but her calm demeanor was not a happy one. As her son became better known and eventually famous, many a visitor attempted to interview Hannah; nearly all of them failed. She was so sparing with her words that no one could compose a satisfactory story about her, and she was so heedless of the reporters' questions that some wondered if she were deaf or mentally deficient. The full truth will probably never be known, but it can safely be said that Grant's mother was a truly internal woman, given to her own thoughts.

If both the Grants and the Simpsons felt a strong desire to excel in the world and to recover a lost material prosperity, much of the burden would have fallen on young Ulysses, the firstborn. Indeed, his father extolled the son from an early age, predicting so many great things for him that neighbors were put off by his talk.

Jesse Root Grant, father of Ulysses S. Grant, was a tanner. Jesse was determined to succeed in life after being abandoned by his father as a child and having to find his own way in the world toiling on farms. Both Jesse and Hannah Grant remained stern and intolerant of people that were not willing to work hard and stay sober.

THE COUNTY SEAT

Point Pleasant is a lovely place in pictures but a very small one, and it is no surprise that the Grant family moved, when Ulysses was about one, to Georgetown. Only 20 miles separated the two places, but Georgetown was much more up-and-coming—it was the seat of Brown County, named for General Jacob Brown of the War of 1812.

Jesse built his growing family a nice two-story house in Georgetown, but young Ulysses, in later days, primarily remembered two things from those early days: one pleasant and the other appalling. He hated his father's tannery. The smell from the chemicals his father used made him feel nauseous, and he wanted nothing to do with the line of work. This did not create hard feelings between father and son, for Jesse was confident that this son, the apple of his eye, would succeed at something in life. The first inkling of that something was apparent from Ulysses's first, and perhaps his greatest, love: horses.

At the age of two, Ulysses was taken to a circus, where his overwhelming desire was to be the child that rode the pony (he did). By the age of three or four, he was playing among the horses of his father's stall, where he seemed immune to the kinds of accidents and injuries suffered by most children. When neighbors expressed concern that the child might be hurt, his parents shrugged this off by saying he would take care of himself. Whether this represented an unusual faith and confidence in their son or a sort of benign form of child neglect, what emerges is a portrait of a rather lonely boy, unhappy with the work done by his father, who began to prefer the company of horses to that of humans.

In *Personal Memoirs*, Grant describes a scene that is revealing of both his nature and of his dealings with others. At the age of 10, Ulysses set his eyes on a special horse in the neighborhood, and he asked his father for the money to purchase it:

> When I got to Mr. Ralston's house, I said to him, 'Papa says I may offer you twenty dollars for the colt, but if you won't take that, I am to offer twenty-two and a half, and if you won't take that, to give you twenty-five.' It would not require a Connecticut man [Yankee] to guess the price finally agreed upon.

Ulysses obtained the horse of his dreams, but he suffered much ridicule from boys in the neighborhood who were not shy in pointing out what a poor horse trader he had become. The episode is small but telling. Ulysses generally loved horses more than people, with a few notable exceptions, and throughout life he remained a poor judge of money and of character—at least in terms of people who had money.

EARLY TRAVELS

"I was already the best-traveled boy in Georgetown, except the sons of one man, John Walker, who had emigrated to Texas with his family, and immigrated back as soon as he had the means to do so." This was how Grant in later years described his great zest for travel.

Perhaps the dislike of his father's tannery drove Ulysses outward; then again, it may have been the cool and reserved nature of his mother. Whichever is true, young Ulysses delighted in moving about. By the age of 12, he was escorting travelers on long horse-and-carriage rides through the country, taking them across flooding rivers and into high hilltops. Travel seemed to hold no fears for Ulysses, probably because it combined horses and movement with his desire to get away from the family home. There is no indication of conflict with his younger siblings—Ulysses seems to have been a good-natured elder brother—but with each passing year he became less and less of his father's favorite. The son who was expected to break all records in the pursuit of money and success was almost allergic to the family business, and Jesse became sterner with each passing season.

Ulysses attended school all along. He later derided the type of compulsory education available in southern Ohio, but in actuality it was neither better nor worse than the schools of Massachusetts, Virginia, or any of the other states at the time. Learning was primarily by repetition; Ulysses later recalled that he recited "A noun is the name of a thing" so many times that he came to believe it. He showed strong aptitude in mathematics, and by his late teenage years, his father began to believe Ulysses might make him proud after all.

One day, on Christmas vacation in the year 1838, Jesse told his son that an opening existed for a local boy to attend the U.S. Military Academy at West Point (the vacancy was created by another boy flunking out). Ulysses's first response was simple—"But I won't go"—and his father's was even more so—"He said he thought I would, and I thought so too, if he did." Today we might call this harsh, but frontier boys of the nineteenth century (when Ohio was still part of the frontier) either obeyed their fathers or ran away from home. Ulysses might have been tempted to run off, but here was an opportunity that allowed him to do so, after a fashion, while seeing some truly new sights. Soon he was bound for the East Coast.

WEST POINT

Ulysses had been around much of Ohio, and he knew something of Kentucky, but New York State and the Hudson River were a far cry from Cincinnati and the Ohio River. He took his time, visiting Simpson relatives along the way. When he arrived at West Point in the summer of 1839, he announced himself ready to take up his cadet duties. It was there, at West Point, that he became, once and for all, Ulysses Simpson Grant. The congressman who had written his letter of recommendation had mistakenly dropped the "Hiram" and added the "Simpson," thinking that the boy must have his mother's family name somewhere in his own. Young Grant attempted to change the spelling and wording, but the officials at West Point absolutely refused. If Congressman Hamer had written it as "Ulysses Simpson Grant," then so it must remain. Grant had never been called "Hiram" very much, and he was not sorry to see that name go. Somewhat to his surprise, his West Point classmates called him "U.S. Grant," which they often shorted to "Sam."

WEST POINT.

The United States Military Academy, or West Point, established in 1802 by Thomas Jefferson, is the oldest academy in the United States. A high number of distinguished American generals have been trained at West Point in four critical areas: intellectual, physical, military, and moral-ethical. Notable graduates have included Ulysses S. Grant, Robert E. Lee, Jefferson Davis, and William T. Sherman, among many others.

Grant lightened up during his West Point years. Never a good "mixer" and certainly not smart when it came to gaining influential and powerful friends, he nevertheless was seen as a good chum and a reliable friend.

Grant was a freshman at West Point when William Tecumseh Sherman (see Chapter Six) was a senior. Likewise, Grant was a senior when Thomas "Stonewall" Jackson was a freshman. Neither of these two men made much of an impression on Grant—nor he on them—but he did know, from his own class, Joseph Jones Reynolds, later a major-general; Rufus Ingalls, later a brigadier general; and Samuel Gibbs French, who, at the time of his death in 1910, was the oldest living West

WEST POINT IN GRANT'S TIME

In 1839, the year Grant arrived, West Point was America's military academy. It had not, however, yet become the place revered by military historians and folklorists alike. The faculty was small, many of the courses were pedestrian in nature, and being a West Point graduate—while prestigious—was not as important as it is today.

The instructors at West Point were mostly enamored of Napoleonic military strategy; they based their classes and readings on studies of the Napoleonic Wars, which raged between 1796 and 1815. A reading knowledge of French, something with which Grant struggled, was a must for understanding the West Point curriculum.

There were teachers of real ability, but they tended to have oversized egos—Dennis Hart Mahan, the father of the even more famous naval writer Alfred Thayer Mahan, is one prime example. Instructors tended to zealously guard their areas of specialty, making it unlikely that those professors and students would ever come into general, uninhibited discussion.

Even given the apparent weaknesses, the Military Academy at West Point was in the midst of building a tradition. In the year Grant arrived as a cadet, there was a small but growing movement in Congress to abolish the Academy; by the time he graduated in 1843, the Academy was clearly there to stay.

Grant expressed mixed feelings about West Point. In letters he wrote home at the time, he extolled the natural beauty of the area and the richness of its history; this, after all, was where Benedict Arnold's infamous treason had taken place. But in letters written many years later, Grant seldom enthused about West Point. On at least one occasion, he spoke of graduating the Academy as a sort of escape from a dreary place.

Point graduate. Just one year ahead of Grant, in the Class of 1842, were William Starke Rosecrans, Abner Doubleday, and James Longstreet, all of whom would receive Civil War laurels, though not all on the same side. Perhaps most important of all, however, was Grant's friendship with his senior-year roommate, Frederick Tracy Dent. It was through Dent that Grant would find his future wife.

Grant did not make much of a splash academically. He graduated 21 in a class of 39. His only sensational moment came in his senior year when he led his favorite horse in a jump that set a record that would last for years to come. Some observers that day came away from the jump thinking that there was more to "Sam" Grant than expected, and everyone hoped he would be posted to the one regiment of dragoons (mounted cavalry) then in existence in the U.S. Army. But the military, in its wisdom (or lack thereof), posted him to the Fifth Infantry regiment as a second lieutenant. Historians often point to the inefficiencies of large bureaucracies; here was a major example of desk officers making a huge mistake, putting the service's best horseman into an infantry regiment. But, as Grant later observed in *Personal Memoirs*, "Man proposes, God disposes."

Love and War

Men heading off to war often court and marry quickly. The former was the case with Ulysses S. Grant (the name that would stick for the rest of his life), but the latter—marriage—was long delayed.

ST. LOUIS

Immediately after graduation, Grant learned that he had been posted to Jefferson Barracks. Then the largest of its kind, Jefferson Barracks was about six miles outside of St. Louis. By now, Grant had overcome his disappointment over being selected for infantry service, and when he left West Point he had a fine, smart-looking lieutenant's uniform. His romantic attachment to military splendor was extremely short-lived, however. As he passed through Cincinnati, Grant rode

Grant, then second lieutenant, is shown in a drawing made shortly after graduating from West Point in 1843. Later in his career, he was sometimes called sloppy in appearance, and even following his promotion, Grant often wore the uniform of a private with the straps of a lieutenant general rather than the ornate uniform of the officers of his day.

proudly, thinking people would admire his military clothing, but a young urchin, barefoot and with pants held up by only one suspender, saw him and called out, "Soldier! Will you work? No sir-ee; I'll sell my shirt first!" This was a small but important incident in Grant's life; almost from that day on he shook off any feeling of self-importance attached to a uniform, and for the rest of his many military years, he would dress "down" rather than "up."

Reporting to Jefferson Barracks, Grant found a large, convivial group of brother officers. He was in the Regular Army now, distinguished from militia groups, but the Army of 1843 was a very chummy place, or at least Grant found it so. Not only was there a relaxed attitude in camp, but Grant received numerous passes for official leave, and he took to visiting the Dent family about five miles away. The parents and siblings of his West Point classmate Frederick Dent lived on an estate they called White Haven, and a haven it became for the young army officer.

Colonel Frederick Dent Sr. was a large, pompous, and rather vain man—the title of colonel was strictly an honorary one given by fellow farmers. A native of Maryland and the owner of nearly 20 slaves, Frederick Dent lived a comfortable but boring life, enlivened only by his large family. His youngest daughter, Emily, was the first to see and take to Lieutenant Grant (she thought him a perfect doll), but her older sister Julia Boggs Dent was the most eligible one at the time.

Solidly built, though in later years she became truly overweight, and equipped with an athletic disposition, Julia became Grant's favorite companion in horse riding. Grant began to extend his visits to the Dent homestead, and he courted Julia, first awkwardly and then passionately. Julia was no beauty; she had a serious twitch to her right eye that no medicine could cure. But she was lively and fun, things Grant hadn't experienced in either of his rather severe parents. As he later expressed it, "my visits became more frequent; they certainly did become more enjoyable." While Grant worked up his nerve to ask Julia's father for her hand, other events intruded on his courtship.

WAR WITH MEXICO

Grant graduated from West Point in 1843, just two years prior to the American annexation of Texas. The Lone Star Republic, as it was called then, had won its independence from Mexico in 1836, and many people had expected that the United States would quickly welcome Texas into the ranks of states. But as it became obvious that Texas would enter as a state that permitted slavery, many Northern senators and representatives opposed the measure. It was not until December 1845 that the Lone Star Republic entered the Union and became known as the Lone Star State.

The government of Mexico—whose constitution was based on the American one—naturally resented this annexation, and both sides threatened to declare war. American president James K. Polk wanted all of Texas, while the Mexican government argued that the pre-annexation boundary had been the Nueces River, not the Rio Grande. To make sure no one would think that he, or the United States, was weak, President Polk ordered about nine-tenths of the entire Regular Army to occupy the land between the Nueces and the Rio Grande.

Receiving his orders to move out, Lieutenant Grant went south to Louisiana, where he and his comrades spent some months at a place they called Camp Salubrity; it was from there that Grant wrote his first earnest love letters to Julia. One of the earliest to survive was dated June 4, 1844, a letter that concluded with a strong expression of passion:

> Julia! I cannot express the regrets that I feel at having to leave Jeff. Bks. [Jefferson Barracks] at the time that I did. I was just learning how to enjoy the place and the Society, at least a part of it.

Grant then drew 21 blank lines in a row on the paper.

> Read these blank lines just as I intend them and they will express more than words—You must not forget to write soon and what to seal with. Until I hear from you I shall be—I don't know what I was going to say—but I reckon it was your most humble and Obt. Friend.
>
> (signed)
> Ulysses S. Grant

Grant was in love at the time he was called to war.

TEXAS AND MEXICO

The Army of Occupation, as the American force was called, proceeded from Louisiana to the southernmost part of Texas in the winter of 1845–1846. In his letters, and later in his memoirs, Grant showed he had little sympathy for his own government and its aims, thinking that the Army of Occupation was there to provoke a war with Mexico. Grant did not share this opinion with his brother officers, but examination of their diaries over the years reveals that many of them felt the same way.

The Mexican-American War began in April 1846, when groups of Mexican cavalrymen crossed the Rio Grande to attack outlying detachments of American soldiers. Grant was asleep when he heard the first guns—Mexican cannon—firing on his location, and for a moment he wondered if he had made the right decision for a career. But the thought soon passed, and days later, Grant participated in the Battles of Palo Alto and Resaca de la Palma. He fought fiercely in the second battle and came off entirely unscathed; some of his comrades were not so fortunate. Years later, when writing his memoirs, Grant expressed the difference between two types of soldiers and, for that matter, men:

> A great many men, when they smell battle afar off, chafe to get into the fray. When they say so themselves they

Grant served in the Mexican-American War (1846–1848) with the rank of lieutenant and got close enough to the front lines to see action, taking part in the Battle of Palo Alto (*above*). He was promoted twice and continued, until his death, to regard it as an unjust war.

> generally fail to convince their hearers that they are as anxious as they would like to believe, and as they approach danger they become more subdued. This rule is not universal, for I have known a few men who were always aching for a fight when there was no enemy near, who were as good as their word when the battle did come. But the number of such men is small.

Grant did not classify himself in either category, but one suspects he was closer to the latter than the former. The boy who used to play fearlessly with the horses in his father's barn had become a man who practiced war without fear—or without any that was noticeable.

The American Army of Occupation won both battles and soon crossed the Rio Grande, heading south; some observers claimed this made them into the Army of Invasion. General Zachary Taylor, commander of the Army of Occupation, was an old soldier with a style that endeared him to his men—they called him "Old Rough and Ready." Grant came to admire his commander, who, he noted, was the antithesis of the smartly uniformed officer. Taylor dressed in civilian-like clothing; sat on his horse sideways, with both feet dangling off one side; and generally cared not a whit for the spit-and-polish military espoused by places like West Point. Making mental notes of his commander, Grant saw that part of Taylor's effectiveness came from his irregularity; here was a general that breakfasted with the troops, rode with them, and acted as if he were only the first among equals. Many years later, the same things would be said of Grant.

Taylor and the American army invaded the Mexican city of Monterrey, beginning a siege that lasted nearly a week. Grant came under fire a number of times, and he acted with the deliberate coolness that was beginning to mark his career. Taylor began to depend on him to the extent that Grant was made a quartermaster, responsible for the supply wagons, munitions, and food for the army. But almost as soon as he had won the approval of one general, Grant and his regiment were transferred to serve under another.

General Winfield Scott was, in style, the antithesis of General Taylor; his men called him "Old Fuss and Feathers." The oldest serving officer in the U.S. Army, Scott had been in important battles during the War of 1812, had helped to suppress the Seminole Rebellion in the 1830s, and was generally considered the most professional of all American military men. Grant had seen Scott before, during a review at West Point, and at the time he thought him the most splendid and commanding of men. Scott's body was old and tired, but his mind was as sharp as ever. Grant came to appreciate Scott's military brilliance, which was exhibited as the American army landed at Vera Cruz and then headed into the Mexican

MEXICAN WAR LESSONS

No one in 1847 thought that the northern and southern parts of the United States would fight a great civil war, but the officers and men of the army that invaded Mexico gained many valuable lessons, some of which were put to use in the later conflict.

The Mexican War showed the wise person that sheer weight of numbers was not as important as in the past; many West Point instructors, feverishly studying the Napoleonic Wars, missed this lesson. Captain Grant and many of his contemporaries, including Robert E. Lee, saw that a smaller body of troops, well supported by light artillery, could defeat a much larger one.

Another lesson had to do with terrain. Napoleon's battles had been fought in well-watered areas of central and western Europe (though his Spanish campaign was an obvious exception), allowing him to draw on the land and its resources. An American army, by contrast, might have to march from the 30th parallel of latitude (Florida) to the 45th (the Canadian border with Vermont).

Disease, too, played a major role in the Mexican War. Far more American soldiers died from cholera and dysentery than from enemy gunfire. This lesson was absorbed by most of the junior American officers, and Civil War armies were held to higher standards of cleanliness and hygiene than those of the Mexican War.

countryside. Though he never came to know Scott in the way he knew Taylor, Grant was astute enough to see that the two men—different in so many ways—shared something in common: They were superb leaders of men.

Grant made many acquaintances and friends along the 200-mile march to Mexico City. Some he had known at West Point, however faintly, and others were first-time meetings. A list of the names of American officers who served on that campaign and who later fought in the Civil War would be long indeed; suffice to say that Grant began or renewed friendships with James Longstreet, Simon Bolivar Buckner, Pierre Beauregard, Thomas "Stonewall" Jackson, and others. Grant did not become close with Captain Robert E. Lee, commander of the engineers, but few men did. Captain Lee, a graduate of the West Point class of 1829, was widely respected and well liked, but he had so grave and serious a demeanor that few people became close to him. One who did was General Scott; he made Lee the chief of scouts, sending him on numerous reconnaissance missions around the countryside.

Thanks to the good scouting, to General Scott's brilliance, and to the valor of thousands of common soldiers, the American army reached the outskirts of Mexico City in September 1847. Two hard-fought battles won the Americans the surrounding areas, and Lieutenant Grant played a gallant role in the battle for Celino Gate—he and his men hoisted a small cannon into a church belfry and used it to command the nearby streets. For this, Grant was mentioned in the official dispatches.

General Scott and his staff entered Mexico City on September 13, 1847; they were the first Americans to occupy a foreign capital. Lieutenant Grant would have been pleased to go home right away, but he was part of the occupation force that remained in Mexico for the next six months while the terms of peace were being decided. One of his letters to

Julia refers both to his struggles and to those of her brother, Frederick:

> Since my last letter to you four of the hardest fought battles that the world ever witnessed have crowned the American arms. But dearly have they paid for it! . . . Among the wounded you will find Fred's name but he is now walking about and in the course of two weeks more will be entirely well. I saw Fred a moment after he received his wound but escaped myself untouched.

Frederick did heal, and as one of the wounded, he reached home before Grant.

But where was home? Grant had not lived with his parents since the spring of 1839. He had been at West Point, at Jefferson Barracks, at Camp Salubrity, and then in Mexico City. Home, he came to feel, was with Julia.

Before leaving for Mexico, Grant had asked Colonel Dent for his daughter's hand. Dent had given his permission, but he was never entirely reconciled to the thought of his beloved, and rather spoiled, daughter marrying an army officer. Grant's future, and especially his income, seemed in doubt, and Colonel Dent wondered if Julia would ever be happy as the wife of an army man. Even so, the magical day arrived.

Recently returned from Mexico, Lieutenant Grant married Julia Boggs Dent on August 22, 1848. James "Pete" Longstreet, later of Confederate fame, was his best man. Julia later described the event in her memoirs:

> My wedding was necessarily a simple one. The season was unfavorable for a large gathering, and our temporary home in St. Louis was small. We were married about eight o'clock, and received during the evening all of our old friends in the city.

On August 22, 1848, Grant married Julia Boggs Dent. Neither of their fathers approved of the match—hers because of Grant's bleak prospects as a career soldier, his because the Dents were slave owners. The couple remained fiercely loyal to each other throughout their lives.

There is, in Mrs. Grant's writing, a yearning for things to be grander, for the home to be a permanent, rather than temporary, one. Yet this beginning had many of the elements that would influence the couple's married life. Their homes would nearly always be temporary ones, and things they hoped would be grand often turned out to be the opposite.

Grant had taken the single most decisive step of his life. Through all the joys and sorrows, victories and changes to come, he would have Julia by his side. One historian has claimed that the two practically became one person over the decades to come.

Depression and Drink

Grant was vulnerable to depression and those feelings led him to drink. Only by realizing just how low he sank in the 1850s can one develop the necessary empathy for a man in deep trouble.

DETROIT AND SACKETS HARBOR

There was no immediate sign of impending trouble. Mr. and Mrs. Grant left St. Louis for a short stay in Bethel, Ohio—Grant's parents had moved yet again—before departing for the James Madison Barracks in Detroit. Hardly had the couple set up house in Detroit, however, when Grant was mistakenly posted to the much more remote Sackets Harbor, on the south side of Lake Erie. On his own, Grant would not have protested (such was his nature), but now he had a wife. She urged him to do so, and before long the couple was posted back in Detroit.

Detroit was a rather small place in 1848, but it was clearly on the way up; anyone with a forward look could see that it would someday become a major center for trade and commerce. Ulysses and Julia were happy enough in Detroit. Their first child, Frederick Dent Grant, was born in 1849. But the U.S. Army decided to send the 4th Regiment to the West Coast, which had boomed ever since the discovery of gold in California in 1848. After some long and earnest discussions, the Grants decided to separate. Ulysses would go west with his regiment and seek to earn extra money on the side; Julia would return to her family at White Haven and await the proper time to join her husband in the West. It was a bad, though understandable, mistake.

CROSSING NICARAGUA

Ulysses Grant and the 4th Regiment sailed from New York City in 1849. The sail down to Central America was uneventful, but it was only the first part of a three-leg journey. There was no Panama Canal in those days so, in order to save time, people shipped to Panama or Nicaragua, crossed the dangerous isthmus, and then sailed up the west coast of Mexico on their way to California.

Grant and his regiment made it to Nicaragua without difficulty, but their crossing of the isthmus was horrific. As one of the regimental quartermasters, Grant saw firsthand how deadly the yellow fever was among the men and how poorly the regiment was equipped to deal with it (the cure for yellow fever was not found until the first decade of the twentieth century). Nearly 100 men, women, and children died on the crossing.

Arriving at San Francisco, Grant followed orders in going to Fort Vancouver on the Columbia River, on the border between Oregon and Washington State. There he spent the next two years, which were among the unhappiest of his entire life.

Grant had come to depend upon Julia, and she upon him. They were a truly devoted couple. He needed her to keep him

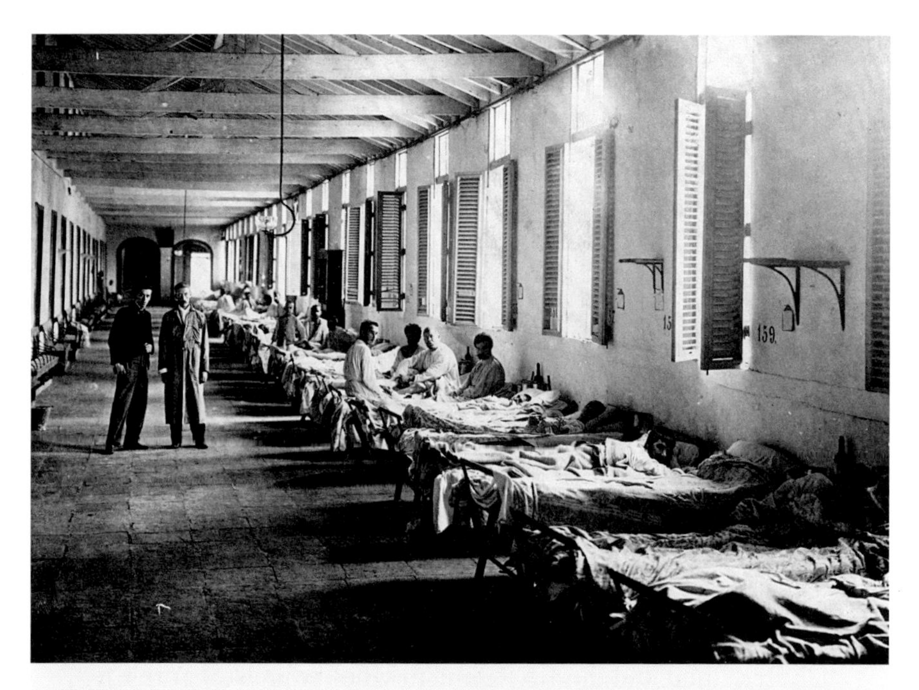

On July 5, 1849, Grant, along with eight companies of the 4th Infantry, headed to Panama. Grant was thankful that Julia and his son remained home, for men, women, and children were stricken with yellow fever, cholera, and other discomforts. Grant helped nurse the sick, like those in this yellow fever hospital, and was rarely able to sleep for long.

"on the wagon," to feel there was a purpose to his life, and she needed him to make her feel that all was right with the world.

The army received the brunt of Grant's anger. Upset by the distance from Julia and from his second child, who was born while he was en route to the West Coast, Grant began to think about resigning from the army. The major difficulty was that "poverty, dire poverty" stared him in the face each time he considered it.

The more he thought about resigning from the army, the more important it was to have another source of livelihood. So, in the winter of 1851, Grant experimented with cutting blocks of ice on the Columbia and shipping them to San Francisco; the scheme was well-founded, but the ice arrived at a time when the market was saturated. Similarly, when Grant experimented with becoming a part owner of a dry-goods store in San Francisco, his business partner absconded with all the funds.

THE LOWEST POINT

Things became even worse in 1853 when Grant was transferred to Fort Humboldt on the northern California coast. The scenery was better there, but the loneliness was terrible, and Grant had a new tormentor in a superior officer who remembered him from his time at Jefferson Barracks in Missouri. Just how much the older and senior-ranking man did to hurt Grant's pride will never be known, but by the spring of 1854, he was dead broke, physically exhausted, and in utter need of a change.

Grant resigned from the U.S. Army with the rank of captain in the spring of 1854.

His father, Jesse, was dismayed to hear the news. He wrote to his congressman, who put him in touch with the U.S. Secretary of War, Jefferson Davis. Jesse implored Davis to grant his son a six-month leave to visit his family and then to reinstate him in the army, but Davis refused. As Davis explained in his letter to Grant's father, Captain Grant had resigned without giving any specific reasons for doing so, and the army already had a surplus of captains and lieutenants.

Grant's homecoming was fraught with difficulty. First there was a steamship voyage from San Francisco to Panama, followed by the dangerous crossing of the isthmus. Delay followed delay before Grant reached New York City that autumn. Hoping against hope that he could collect a debt from an old army friend, he went from Manhattan to Sackets Harbor, only to find that the friend was on leave. At one of the lowest points of his entire life, Grant returned to Manhattan, where he was able to borrow money from an old West Point comrade, Simon Bolivar Buckner, and to obtain a loan, long-distance, from his father. By the time he reached White Haven for an emotional reunion with his wife and children, Grant was at the end of his rope.

HARDSCRABBLE

Julia took her husband back (he seemed to have had some doubts that she would), and the couple resumed their happy married life, complete with their third and fourth children, who arrived in 1855 and 1858. A devoted father, Grant played with his children and was much better and kinder to them than his own father had been to him. But, try as he might, Grant could not escape an overwhelming sense of failure.

By 1858, Grant's younger brothers were successful partners in the tanning business with their father. Old Jesse was now worth

GRANT AND DRINK

One of the most lasting impressions of Ulysses S. Grant is that he was a drunk, often on the edge of sanity. There is more than a kernel of truth to the notion.

Grant grew up in a teetotaling family (absolute abstinence from alcoholic beverages), but he recorded, in his memoirs, having an occasional drink. It must be said that there was absolutely no record of drink on his West Point record; given the number of demerits he accumulated through other things, one or two drinking occasions would have led to his being expelled.

It is hard to say whether Grant drank during the Mexican War, but it is safer to claim that, once married, he became more susceptible than before. Partly this was due to the pressure of providing for his growing family; another part had to do with the long absences from Julia and the children. Undoubtedly, Grant did drink during the lonely nearly $100,000, and he could proudly claim he had earned every dime. By contrast, his eldest son, once the apple of his eye, had become the family loser.

In 1856, Grant built a house several miles outside of St. Louis. Tired of living under his father-in-law's roof, he fashioned a frame building that was larger than the one in which he had been born but was much cruder. Naming it "Hardscrabble," he moved the family there that summer and spent the autumn and winter cutting and carting loads of wood into the city. Some former army officers were shocked to find a disheveled and

times at Vancouver and Fort Humboldt, but the occasional references to his having stumbled and fallen on the parade ground appear to be exaggerated.

Grant stayed "on the wagon" more during the Civil War than at any other time. Impressed with his responsibilities and conscious that he was sending men off to their possible deaths, Grant only had one major slip—during the trying Vicksburg campaign. Generally there was little rumor or report of scandal during his Civil War years.

It is impossible to say whether Grant took up drinking again while in the White House, for no correspondents spent time within the Executive Mansion, but numerous political advertisements and cartoons did display him as tipping the bottle for hours on end. It is worth stating, for the record, that whatever alcohol did to Grant—and most modern psychologists would consider him an alcoholic—he did not take it out on the people around him.

In September 1856, the Grants lived in the house above, which Grant built himself. It was so crude that the family named it Hardscrabble. They lived there for only three months, until Julia's father asked the Grants to move to White Haven after the death of Julia's mother in January 1857.

depressed Grant standing by a large cart in the middle of St. Louis. They tried to press money on him, but he always turned it down, saying that everything was fine.

REAL ESTATE

By 1859, Grant had no money and nowhere to go. The only opportunity that presented itself was work with his wife's cousin, Harry Boggs, as a collector of rents in St. Louis. Grant made a go of this work, but his heart was not in it, and by 1860, he had decided to swallow his pride and ask his overbearing father for a job.

Jesse always had been a hard man, and he may have delighted in saying "I told you so," but he gave his prodigal son one more chance. In the spring of 1860, the Grants moved to Galena, Illinois, on the Mississippi River, where Grant would be a junior clerk in a store managed by his younger brother Orville. To say he had come down in the world would be an understatement.

He, a graduate of West Point, a minor hero in the Mexican War, now was working where he might have started life all those years ago— in one of his father's tannery shops.

He would not remain there long.

THE SECESSION CRISIS

Until the year 1860, there was little in Grant's life to suggest a political interest. He later admitted that he never voted for president until 1852, and in 1856 he supported James Buchanan, the compromise candidate, in a year when a strong leader was needed. But as the great crisis of 1860 began, Grant showed signs of life.

In November 1860, Abraham Lincoln was elected president without the majority—only about 40 percent—of the popular vote. Lincoln won handily in the electoral college, thanks to a four-way election among the Northern Democrats, Southern Democrats, the new Republican Party (Lincoln's), and the new Constitutional Union Party. Lincoln was not a full-fledged abolitionist, but Southern Democrats heartily disliked and mistrusted him. Believing he would try to free the slaves, members of the Southern Democratic Party formed caucuses in the fall of 1860, and in December the South Carolina convention made the momentous step of seceding from the United States.

Six other Southern states followed suit, and by March 4, 1861, the day Lincoln was inaugurated, seven states had left the Union, creating nothing short of a constitutional crisis. Many a man, Northern and Southern, believed such a crisis could be the making of him. Many a man hastened to the battlefield, only to be disillusioned, to be wounded, or to find an early grave. But some men did thrive under the pressure of the great Civil War.

Grant was one of those men who did. The reasons remain a little murky, even today, but there is no doubt that he thought like a Union man and acted like one, and that fighting for the Union would be the making of his name and fame.

A New Life

Almost everyone who has spent time examining Grant's life has marveled at the change that took place in the spring of 1861. A career soiled by failure suddenly turned into one marked by determination and vigor.

WAR BEGINS

The American Civil War began on April 12, 1861, when Confederate guns opened fire on Fort Sumter, a Union post, in the harbor of Charleston, South Carolina. Though only one man was killed in the engagement, which ended with Sumter's surrender, the great contest between North and South, feared and dreaded for so long, had suddenly arrived.

Grant left no doubt as to where he stood. Galena, Illinois, and the surrounding area received the news of Fort Sumter five days

Decades of strife between North and South finally came to a head on April 12, 1861, when Confederate artillery fired shots on Fort Sumter, initiating the American Civil War. Shortly after, President Lincoln put out a call for volunteers, and Grant helped recruit and train volunteers in Illinois. Union forces would try to take back the fort for nearly four years.

after its surrender, and Grant made up his mind at once, as shown by a letter he wrote to his father-in-law:

> Dear Sir—
>
> The times are indeed startling, but now is the time, particularly in the border Slave states, for men to prove their love of country. I know it is hard for men [like yourself] to apparently work with the Republican party, but now all party distinctions should be lost sight of, and every true patriot be for maintaining the integrity of the glorious old Stars and Stripes, the Constitution and the Union.

Very likely Grant had two reasons for writing in such a tone. First, he was a Union man, born and bred, and his West Point years had made him even more so. Second, he had long chafed under the pretensions and superior feelings of his father-in-law, a man who did little work in life but who looked down on his son-in-law's failures in business and farming. For the first time in their relationship, Grant had the upper hand, the moral high ground, and he made sure that Dent was aware of it. Grant continued:

> In all this I can but see the doom of Slavery. The North does not want, nor will they want, to interfere with the institution; but they will refuse for all time to give it protection unless the South shall return soon to their allegiance.

Grant was ahead of his time, if just by a few months, in this statement. Many a Union man went to fight the battles of 1861 with the notion that the war was strictly about the issue of union versus disunion. Grant was not yet a true abolitionist—he did not call for the end of slavery—but he accurately saw that the war would lead to the demise of the institution.

REGULARS AND VOLUNTEERS

Almost as soon as the war began, the men of Galena held a meeting to discuss their contribution to the Union effort. Though Grant had lived in the town for less than a year, he chaired the meeting because he had been a captain in the Regular (which is to say, the commissioned) Army until his resignation in 1854.

Galena decided to raise a company of infantry. Grant could have been its captain, but he declined the opportunity because he felt, as someone who had once been a commissioned officer in the Regular Army, that he merited being jumped to major or colonel. Grant soon regretted this decision, for no one in the Regular Army showed much interest in an old comrade, especially one whose record was tarnished by his sudden resignation in peacetime.

SLAVE-OWNER GRANT

One of the most astonishing incongruities of Grant's life is that he was, however briefly, the owner of an African-American slave.

Grant had married Julia, knowing quite well that she came from a slave-owning family. At the peak of their prosperity, the Dents owned as many as 20 slaves, and Julia's memoir, written many years later, sang the praises and joys of having so many surrogate sisters among the "darkies," as she called them.

Grant himself came from a family that thoroughly disapproved of slaveholding. Ohio businessmen like his father tended to oppose the institution on principle, but they did not believe in violent action to overthrow it. Neither in his letters nor in his personal memoirs does Grant describe his own feelings toward the institution, but in 1857, when he was near the end of his resources, he accepted the gift of one of his father-in-law's slaves.

William Jones, a 35-year-old African American, became Grant's assistant, both in working on the Hardscrabble farm and in the carting of wood. Two years later, in 1859, Grant went to the St. Louis court and officially set William free, though without any compensation whatsoever (biographers have long commented that Grant could have used the $50 manumission fee that was standard at the time). Even so, the remarkable incongruity remains—the man who was second only to Lincoln in his influence over the freeing of 4 million black slaves, had himself owned one just a few years before.

Leaving Galena, Grant went to Springfield, Illinois, the state capital, where he helped drill the 4th Volunteer Infantry Regiment without any rank or any pay. Grant had never been very effective at cultivating influential friends, but he tried, in the spring of 1861, to get officers of the Regular Army to pay attention to him. He traveled around Illinois and even ventured into northern Kentucky, seeking old friends and possible new ones, but nothing worked until the end of May when he was rather suddenly appointed colonel of the 7th District Regiment of Illinois Volunteers.

Scheduled to deliver his first speech to his new regiment, Colonel Grant waited while two political leaders preceded him. One was a fine speaker, full of energy, and the other was rather lackluster. Finally came the moment for the new colonel.

Grant knew that many of the newly enlisted volunteers did not have the stomach for a long fight. Like many men at the start of a war, they assumed the enemy would be quickly beaten so they could go home. Grant also knew that some of these volunteers were already weary of the rules of military camp and were looking for any excuse to desert.

So, when it came time for him to speak, Grant stood up and called out rather sharply, "Men, go to your quarters!"

They did. Whether there was some magic in Grant's stern and simple command or whether his men had been influenced by the two former speakers is hard to say, but nearly all the men tamely went to their quarters, bunks, and tents. The 7th Illinois Volunteers was a unit, there to stay.

Much has been made of the remarkable simplicity of Grant's speeches and the effect they often had upon soldiers. From his letters, we know that he had a developed mind, that he could express detailed concepts on paper as well as anyone. But when it came to public speaking, he much preferred the short and simple.

FIRST MOVES

As colonel and leader of a regiment, Grant now was in the greatest position of responsibility of his life. Keenly aware that his Mexican War experience had not entailed sending men into combat, Grant approached his first conflicts gingerly, but once he found his footing, he became as bold as any officer in the Union armies.

Grant's regiment moved to Cairo, Illinois, the place where the Ohio River flows into the Mississippi. This river junction was vital to the Union cause and would have been extremely advantageous to the Confederates if they had arrived first. Not content with merely holding this place, Grant responded to commands that sent him and his regiment into eastern Missouri, looking for a Confederate force of similar size and configuration. Approaching the spot the Confederates held, Grant felt an extreme anxiety, a sense of being unready for this test. But his men crested the brow of a hill to discover that the Confederates had struck their tents and disappeared. Grant later wrote that, in that moment, he realized that his Confederate counterpart was as afraid of him as he had been of the Confederates. From that moment on, Grant approached battle with an increasing sense of confidence.

Grant's campaign in Missouri resulted in only one large engagement, the Battle of Belmont, but that, plus increased attention to his Mexican War record, resulted in his being named one of 26 brand-new brigadier generals of volunteer infantry. The promotion came in August, filling Grant with elation. Just four months before, he had been a rundown, middle-aged failure; now he was a one-star general, leading Union troops in the field.

Kentucky

Early in the great conflict, President Lincoln confided to a friend that he hoped the Almighty was on his side, but that he knew that he must have Kentucky. With his usual intuitive sense, Lincoln saw that controlling the border states of Kentucky, Missouri, Maryland, and Delaware was one of the great keys to victory or defeat.

Grant's infantry regiment moved into northern Kentucky in the winter of 1862. The state was about equally divided between Union and Confederate sympathizers, and the governor and legislature were committed to neutrality, but anyone possessing a strategic eye could see that Kentucky would be a major battleground. Whoever controlled the major rivers—the Kentucky and Cumberland, especially—would be well positioned to hold the state and thereby prolong the war.

Donelson and Henry

The Confederates entered Kentucky from the south while Grant and other Union commanders came from the north. By January 1862, the Confederates were ensconced at Forts Henry and Donelson, both on the Tennessee River.

Marching south, Grant was well aware of his foes. In particular, he knew that they were led by General Simon Bolivar Buckner, a friend from West Point who had lent Grant money at a particularly low period of his life during the summer of 1854. Knowing the mettle of the man who opposed him helped Grant shape his own strategy.

In coordination with a flotilla of Union gunboats commanded by Colonel Andrew Foote, Grant fought his way to Fort Henry, surprising its defenders. Many scrambled to safety just in time, but they had nowhere to run except to Fort Donelson, 15 miles to the east. Another type of commander—even the best ones—might have paused to rest on his laurels, but Grant pushed on, and by mid-February he had his old West Point friend and about 15,000 Confederates under siege at Fort Donelson.

General Buckner and Grant had been friends at West Point and during the Mexican War. Neither had expected to be vaulted to the rank of brigadier general so early in the new conflict, though each may have harbored secret hopes. Just as Grant remembered the friendly and helpful Buckner, so did the Confederate general remember the easygoing Grant from their West Point days. Believing that Grant had him cornered with no hope of relief, Buckner sent a letter under a flag of truce, asking

In this painting, Grant (center, on horseback) looks over Fort Donelson. Fort Donelson was the North's first major victory during the Civil War. The capture of the fort opened the Cumberland River—the heart of Confederate country—for invasion and elevated Grant from an unproven, unknown soldier to the rank of major general. Grant earned the nickname "Unconditional Surrender" Grant.

what terms he might expect from his former Regular Army comrade. He received a curt, crisp answer:

> No terms except an unconditional and immediate surrender can be accepted. I propose to move immediately upon your works.

Those 19 words became the most famous ever to issue from Grant's pen. His men soon began to call him "Unconditional Surrender" Grant.

Today, with the knowledge of how fierce and deadly the Civil War became, we might think little of such a stern demand. But the Civil War was less than a year old, and former members of the Regular Army expected to treat each other gently. Not so with Grant; he had made up his mind about the righteousness of the conflict and the need for severity. He had his way. Buckner and about 15,000 Confederates laid down their arms in the first surrender of a major army in the war.

Shiloh

In the immediate aftermath of Forts Henry and Donelson, Grant became the first significant hero for the Union cause. Generals commanding on the Eastern Front, including Irwin McDowell and George B. McClellan, had larger bodies of troops than Grant, but they had not accomplished anything as large as the capture of 15,000 Confederates. By the spring of 1862, Grant had become a brevet major general (*brevet* was a temporary designation, and eventually he would return to brigadier general).

That spring, Grant and his men pushed down the Cumberland River to invade Louisiana. They made steady progress, in part because of the presence of Union gunboats on the river. Grant did not know—and his scouts failed to discover—that a large Confederate Army was hastening north to confront him.

Alarmed by Grant's sudden success and by the relative ease with which the Union had secured Kentucky, Southern leaders put together an army to move north from Corinth and surprise an unsuspecting Grant. Albert Sidney Johnston, a member of the West Point class of 1826 and a hero of the Mexican War, led the conglomerate of Confederate forces. The collision took place on Sunday, April 7.

Fought near the banks of the Tennessee River, the Battle of Shiloh was, by far, the most savage encounter yet seen in the great conflict. The Confederates attacked at midmorning, throwing Grant and his men into confusion; in one of his rare miscalcu-

The bloodiest battle at the time was fought during the Battle of Shiloh, April 6–7, 1862. Total casualties represented more than the American Revolutionary War, the War of 1812, and the Mexican-American War combined. Grant's reputation suffered and calls for his removal overwhelmed President Lincoln, who continued to stand by him. Today, Grant is recognized for having clear judgment under stress and the ability to see the big picture that ultimately resulted in victory.

lations, Grant had not ordered his men to dig trenches around his positions. The Confederates fought with a controlled fury that was soon equaled by desperate Union men fighting to hold their ground. By early afternoon, the battlefield had become treacherous in more ways than one: Men literally slipped and tripped on blood-soaked patches of grass.

Confederate general Albert Sidney Johnston was killed in the early afternoon as he was close to celebrating what appeared to be victory. The Confederates had driven the Union men back all along the line, and they threatened to push them into a swampy area that might ensure their destruction. But stubborn Union defenders managed to hang on to the area called Sunken Lane, and by later afternoon, the Union lines held, however tenuously.

Union reinforcements came in throughout the night. Steamboats brought in supplies as well as men, and by morning Grant felt more confident about the battle's result. Some of his aides asked if they should begin to withdraw, to which Grant replied that he would attack and whip the Confederates.

Attack?

Grant's army had suffered from almost 15,000 men being killed, wounded, or missing; the Confederates had equal casualties, but Grant had no way of knowing that. Yet, on the morning of April 7, Grant attacked the Confederates and found them in serious disarray. General Johnston had been the heart and soul of that army's offense, and his replacement had no stomach for a second day's battle, so Grant and the Union ended up in possession of the field. This did not mean Grant was spared criticism.

When Northern newspapers reported the butcher's bill (the number of killed, wounded, and missing), a howl went up in many Northern cities. People declared that Grant was a butcher and that he should be replaced. It is true that Grant had done a poor job of stationing his men in the days prior to the Battle of Shiloh, but he also was not credited with having maintained his composure, having rallied his men, and having repulsed the Confederate attack.

Grant kept his head low for the next two months. He retained the rank of major general and still was a major part of the Union leadership in the west, yet he did his best to keep out of the public eye. For a time he was under the close supervision of General William H. Halleck—a desk-type general whom Grant disliked—but Halleck was called to Washington to be chief of staff, and by the autumn of 1862 Grant was his own man once more. That was fortunate, because he was about to take on one of the toughest challenges of all: a city on a high bluff overlooking the Mississippi.

Father of Waters

Grant had grown up on and near the Ohio River and had gone to West Point, which was on the Hudson. From his time at Jefferson Barracks, he knew the Missouri and Mississippi rivers, and his campaigns to capture Forts Henry and Donelson made him aware of the Tennessee and Cumberland. There was one more great Confederate stronghold in the western theatre, and it became Grant's job to free the lower Mississippi from Southern control.

GEOGRAPHY

Today's visitor to Vicksburg, Mississippi, finds a town—not large enough to be called a city—that truly celebrates its Civil War past. He or she does not find the quiet hush of battlegrounds like Bull Run and Gettysburg; rather, the tourist encounters miniature Confederate flags and military regalia sold on the street. More than any other Southern city or town—even Richmond or Atlanta—Vicksburg remains alive to its Confederate heritage.

Vicksburg sits on a narrow cliff, perched about 200 feet above the east bank of the Mississippi, which makes a mighty upside-down U-turn just before the town. Guns placed on that cliff could sweep the breadth of the river, and the Confederates were experts at using the terrain, placing sharpened stakes and other obstacles at certain points in the river. Furthermore, the Yazoo River, which empties into the Mississippi about two miles north of Vicksburg, creates a delta, which made it nearly impossible to assail the town on its northern side. This was the place Grant had to capture.

COMMAND CONFUSION

In the summer of 1862, when Grant's reputation was at a low point, one of his brigadier generals, John McClernand, went to Washington to propose himself as the conqueror of Vicksburg. Having the advantage of personally knowing President Lincoln—they both hailed from Springfield, Illinois—McClernand won a tentative concession from the president and from the secretary of war: They let McClernand raise troops in Illinois for a special campaign against Vicksburg. At no time did Lincoln or Edwin Stanton, the secretary of war, suggest that McClernand would be "jumped up" in rank or come to supersede Major General Grant, but McClernand was enough of an opportunist to feel this might happen.

Realizing that McClernand was ambitious enough to try to overshadow him, Grant stepped up his own preparations. Given enough time, he might have found a way to circumvent Vicksburg's formidable defenses, but the anxiety McClernand gave him pushed Grant to rashness. He allowed Brigadier General William Tecumseh Sherman to make a sudden attack

At the time of his selection as brigadier general, John McClernand's sole military experience consisted of a short stint as a volunteer staff officer during the Black Hawk War. McClernand made many mistakes as corps commander but he also showed skill on several occasions, including helping to prevent a near-total tragedy at Shiloh.

on Vicksburg's north side; the result was a disaster, with nearly 1,000 Union casualties.

FIGHTING THE RIVER

Grant made his move late in the winter of 1862–1863. About 40,000 troops were ferried to the west side of the Mississippi River, where Grant led them in a forced march south. All the while, General Sherman made demonstrations as if to attack Vicksburg; this distraction allowed Grant and his men to move undetected.

WILLIAM T. SHERMAN

The names of Sherman and Grant are forever linked because of their close friendship and their agreement on the manner of prosecuting the war. Numerous other Union generals equaled or even surpassed them in tactical brilliance, but not one came close to their idea of "total war."

Born in Lancaster, Ohio, in 1820, Sherman was two years older than Grant and was ahead of him at West Point. Sherman served in California during the Mexcian War and, like Grant, had little skill at business, although he spent some time in banking. When the war began, Sherman moved quickly to the rank of brigadier general, and he became Grant's most trusted subordinate.

Sherman played number two to Grant's number one in 1862 and 1863, but when Grant became general in chief of all the Union armies, he made Sherman commander in the west. As such, Sherman led the Union forces all

At about the same time, Rear Admiral Dixon Porter undertook one of the most daring ventures of the war. Union steamboats existed in large supply, but virtually all of them were north, not south, of Vicksburg, so on the night of April 16, Porter ran almost his entire fleet down and past the Confederate defenses. Knowing the Confederate gunners would aim for his magazines, Porter concealed them with bales of hay. The ruse worked—only one steamboat was sunk in the daring nighttime run. The next morning, Porter had his whole fleet on the southern side of the town, ready to support Grant.

the way to Atlanta, capturing it just in time to ensure President Lincoln's re-election in November 1864. From there, Sherman pressed on to Charleston and Savannah, cutting a swath of destruction across the Southern countryside. Sherman accepted the surrender of General Joseph E. Johnston two weeks after Grant accepted Lee's at Appomattox.

Grant and Sherman remained close when the war ended, and as president in 1869, Grant named Sherman as his secretary of war. The two men did have controversy in their relationship, which cooled markedly during the 1870s, but on the surface they still appeared as comrades-in-arms. Republican Party elders wanted Sherman to run for the presidency in 1880, but he squashed their hopes by declaring, "If nominated, I will not run; if elected, I will not serve." Those who study Sherman's career sometimes conclude that his witnessing Grant's difficulties in office made him certain he wanted to avoid being placed in the Oval Office himself.

The Union men made a strong and fast march south to a place called "Hard Times" on the west side of the great river. There were Confederates on the eastern side, but Grant crossed just the same, scattering his outnumbered foes in a daring move. For almost the first time in the whole campaign, Grant stood on hard, dry land; he and his men had passed through innumerable swamps and thickets on the way. Stationed 20 miles south of Vicksburg, Grant now had some choices about how to maneuver.

The biggest trouble lay in the area of supplies. Grant had twice crossed the Mississippi on his way to Grand Gulf. His hard-bitten men were able to do this, but quartermasters and supply wagons could not. Logic dictated that Grant should fall south to rendezvous with Union forces coming from New Orleans, but logic did not rule the day. Necessity did. In late April, Grant deliberately cut himself off from supplies, leading his men into enemy territory with no certain hope of finding food. He, and they, would live off the land.

THE CAMPAIGN

By the end of April, Grant was on the move. He had nearly 50,000 men, against whom were arrayed about an equal number of Confederates. But, unlike his foe, Grant had his force entirely concentrated.

Confederate general John Pemberton—whom Grant had known in Mexico—commanded the Vicksburg garrison, and General Joseph E. Johnston (not to be confused with Albert Sidney Johnston) had a relief force about 50 miles from the town. Marching rapidly, Grant positioned himself between them, and he defeated Johnston's men in a sharp engagement in Jackson, Mississippi.

Pemberton brought his army out from Vicksburg to deploy in Grant's rear, but Grant had him shadowed on his march. By the time the two armies collided at Champions Hill, the Union force was larger and displayed higher morale. The battle was hard-fought, but Grant's men held the advantage throughout, and by nightfall, Pemberton's entire army was on the run. Had Grant held any reserve with which to exploit his victory, the campaign might have ended on the spot. Instead, it continued, carrying Grant to the very gates of Vicksburg.

So far in his career, Grant had captured Forts Henry and Donelson. Those places had fallen to him through a combination of rapid movement and quick thinking on his part. But Vicksburg was more strongly defended, and the Confederates within its walls knew they were the last hope for the Southern cause on the Western Front. General Joe Johnston was not far off—though he was contained by Grant's outer defenses—and there were rumors that the Confederate high command in Richmond would send a massive relief army. This might have happened if Robert E. Lee had not invaded Pennsylvania in June—the Eastern Front needed every man it could find.

Grant had prevailed through audacity time and again, so he decided to launch a quick assault on Vicksburg, hoping to surprise or overawe its defenders. Nearly 1,000 Union men were killed or wounded or went missing in that fatal attempt, which showed once and for all that Vicksburg was not the same as Forts Donelson or Henry. Though Grant ached to have the matter over and done with, he settled down to a protracted siege, something that could not fail.

Grant's bold risk in marching beyond his supply lines had paid rich dividends. Mississippi had proven richer than Grant had hoped, and his men lived off the fat of the land while General Pemberton's defenders grew more ragged and weary by the day. Grant made occasional demonstrations of his intent to attack, but in reality he counted on his heavy artillery to batter the town into submission.

VICTORY

Confederate general John Pemberton remembered Grant from the Mexican War; the two were graduates of West Point, separated by two years. Pemberton knew better than to rely on this, for he, like everyone else, knew what Grant had said to General Simon Bolivar Buckner in 1862. Pemberton, nevertheless, held out hope he might obtain better terms from Grant, and toward that end he began negotiations on the first of July 1863, thinking that the upcoming Fourth of July would make the Union general more willing to compromise.

GRANT'S HORSES

Horses were central to Grant's life and career. Though he lived long enough to see the advent of the locomotive and the appearance of the telegraph, Grant remained very much an eighteenth-century person in his soul. Horses, the lifeblood of transportation, were his means of getting around.

When he entered the war as a colonel of volunteers, Grant received a gift of a black horse named Jack. This was followed by another gift, a thoroughbred named Egypt, in honor of that section of southern Illinois. But the greatest moment in Grant's equestrian life came in the winter of 1863-1864. Some weeks after winning the Battle of Chattanooga, Grant was in St. Louis visiting his eldest son, who was very ill (happily, he recovered). While there, Grant received a rather mysterious letter from a stranger who begged him to come to a nearby hotel, as he had something to give him. That something turned out to be a magnificent war horse, a true thoroughbred, whom Grant named Cincinnati. Whether this suggested a connection with the Ohio city of the same name or whether it was connected with the Cincinnatus Society, founded in 1783, is impossible to say. But whatever the reason for his name, Cincinnati had

In *Personal Memoirs*, Grant rejected the idea as utter foolishness, saying that his motivation was due to his desire to end the siege quickly, rather than any need to accomplish something prior to the Fourth of July. The fact remains that the surrender was negotiated on July 3, and that the Confederate garrison—over 30,000 men strong—opened the gates and doors of Vicksburg on July 4, making it a memorable holiday indeed. By

General Grant with one of his horses.

an illustrious pedigree; he had been sired by a horse named Lexington, the most famous racehorse of the day.

Grant and Cincinnati became inseparable over the next two years. Just about the only other person to mount Cincinnati was President Lincoln, who, to Grant's surprise, had no difficulty controlling the spirited animal. When Robert E. Lee went to Appomattox Court House he rode Traveler, and when Grant rode to meet him, he was atop Cincinnati.

sheer coincidence, the three-day Battle of Gettysburg (July 1–3, 1863) had ended just one day earlier, making this an unusually joyous time for Northerners. General George Meade had defeated Lee at Gettysburg, but Meade never caught on with newspaper reporters, whom he detested, or with the public as a whole. Grant became the hero of the day, of the month, and indeed, of the entire year.

President Lincoln recognized Grant's signal accomplishment both in a letter to the general and in a letter to a friend in which he expressed his great pleasure that the "Father of Waters again goes unvexed to the sea."

TENNESSEE

Just two months after Grant's Vicksburg victory, a Union army was badly beaten at the Battle of Chickamauga in south-central Tennessee. The Union force managed to escape destruction only by holding out in the railroad town of Chattanooga. Not surprisingly, Grant was called to the rescue.

Traveling by railroad, Grant was astonished to find the Union forces practically under siege at Chattanooga. The numbers against them were not overwhelming; in fact, they were far from it. The Confederates held most of the high ground, however, and they were intent on starving out the Union garrison, which would have made an excellent turnabout after the loss of Vicksburg.

Grant now was a major general in the Regular Army, something for which he had yearned. Though he was the overall commander of the campaign to liberate Chattanooga, Grant was able to stand back from the fray and allow lesser-ranked men, like Generals Thomas and Rosecrans, to conduct the actual fighting. There was a very tense moment, in the Battle of Lookout Mountain, when Grant suddenly realized that Thomas's men were surging up a set of hills without receiving orders, but both he and Thomas were pleasantly surprised when the result was a complete victory. The Confederates were pushed off the hills, Chattanooga was fully freed, and the Union was given the initiative in the west, something it would never release for the duration of the war.

Grant was not at his best in the Chattanooga campaign. He suffered from a bad injury sustained in the summer. But when the news of his victory reached the Northern cities, his name was the one on everyone's lips. Whether they called him "Hiram Ulysses," "Ulysses S.," "Sam," or "Unconditional Surrender," Grant had become a household name in the United States.

The Wilderness and the Crater

March 8, 1864, a Tuesday, was a rainy day in Washington, D.C. The desk clerk at the Willard Hotel—Washington's finest—told a rather rumpled and tired-looking man that all he had available was a room on the third floor. That was fine, the answer came. The middle-aged man and his teenage son began ascending the stairs while the desk clerk looked at the register to see that it was "U.S. Grant and son."

THE HIGHEST RANK

Grant became a major general in the summer of 1863, but something even grander was in store for the conqueror of Vicksburg. During the winter of 1863–1864, Congress passed, and President Lincoln signed, legislation creating the rank of lieutenant general and commander of all the Union armies—something not seen since the time of George Washington.

Grant was becoming accustomed to fame, but even he was taken aback by the symbolism, as well as the high salary. Just three years ago he had been working in his father's tanning shop in Galena, Illinois; now he was honored as the nation's greatest military leader since Washington. When he unceremoniously checked into the Willard Hotel, the clerk spread the news that U.S. Grant had come, and people flocked to see the famous general. A legend was beginning to grow.

THE CHALLENGE

Grant met with President Lincoln in March 1864. Lincoln expressed great confidence in his newfound general, saying he did not need, or wish, to know the details—he trusted Grant to carry out the action that was needed. To both men it was clear that winning a major battle or two, or even capturing the Confederate capital, would not be sufficient. Grant needed to drive the Army of Northern Virginia—which had in turn bedeviled Generals McDowell, McClellan, Pope, Burnside, Hooker, and Meade—into submission. Perhaps it was because they were both Midwesterners, but Lincoln and Grant thought alike on this matter. Victory had to be total.

As commander of all Union armies, Grant detailed his most trusted subordinate, William Tecumseh Sherman, to invade the South from Tennessee. While Sherman moved in a diagonal direction, headed south-by-southeast, Grant would go straight south from Washington, D.C. to tackle Lee and the Army of Northern Virginia.

FIRST MOVES

In May 1864, Grant led the Army of the Potomac, 110,000-men strong, south from Washington, D.C. The Army, which had fought in numerous campaigns, was in the best fighting shape ever; its officers and men were confident they would lick the Army of Northern Virginia this time around.

In that same month, Robert E. Lee brought the Army of Northern Virginia north; Lee knew that Grant and his subordinate generals were more thorough and determined than previous Union leaders, and he wished to deal them a major blow at the outset. The Army of Northern Virginia had 70,000 men in its ranks, but only about 50,000 were in top condition—Lee and his men had suffered badly during the winter months when the declining Confederate economy was unable to provide them with sufficient supplies.

The two armies clashed at a place called The Wilderness. Just south of the Rappahannock River was an area the Confederates knew well and the Yankees knew to a certain extent. The terrible Battle of Chancellorsville had been fought there in 1863; it was one that the Confederates had won by a large margin.

Grant's Union forces ran smack into Lee's Confederates as soon as they entered The Wilderness. Sudden sporadic shots of rifles and muskets gave way to an absolute crescendo of firings of sidearms, long weapons, and artillery; many officers claimed they had never heard the like before. The Union forces fought stubbornly, and there were times when it seemed they would break through holes in the Confederate lines, but each and every time Lee plugged them with a reserve, often one consisting of Texas ranchers. The fighting broke off at dusk, but the horrors of war were compounded by terrible screams heard through the night—flames in the underbrush led to wounded men being consumed by fire, and their screams went on all night long.

Grant attacked on the second day with much the same result. On the third day, the two armies stopped, exhausted from their efforts.

Grant had seen war before. He had been in Mexico, had commanded outside of Forts Henry and Donelson, and had led the remarkable campaign that captured Vicksburg. But he had

In rough terrain that encompassed more than 70 square miles, the Battle of the Wilderness was fought between Grant's Army of the Potomac and Lee's Confederate Army of Northern Virginia. Both armies suffered heavy casualties and the battle is usually considered a draw.

seen nothing like this. About 13,000 Union men were killed or wounded or went missing in the terrible three-day battle. Southern losses were not as high, but the man-poor Southern forces could spare those men even less. It was time to turn around, to return to Washington, and to think of some other plan for the Army of the Potomac. Most people, including officers, newspapermen, and politicians agreed on this. But Grant did not. Just one day after the Battle of the Wilderness ended, he faked a maneuver, surprised Lee, and moved rapidly to the Southerner's right flank. Caught off guard, Lee had to fall back to defend his position, and Grant suddenly made his way out of The Wilderness and into the light of clear day, emerging at Spotsylvania Court House.

Another battle, not quite as large as The Wilderness, took place at Spotsylvania. Grant came away with thousands of casualties. Again there were calls for him to be replaced, but Grant continued on, apparently unfazed. In a telegram to the secretary of war, Grant spelled out his philosophy: "I propose to fight it out along this line if it takes all summer."

Today, with our knowledge of modern warfare, Grant's move seems obvious. Naturally a commander with superior manpower would continue the fight—eventually he would grind his opponent into the dust. But Americans in 1864 were not the Americans of 1944; the public was not inured to news accounts of terrible casualties. Many politicians and newsmen complained bitterly of "Grant the Butcher" who, they claimed, was leading a generation of young men to slaughter.

President Lincoln remained solidly, indeed completely, in General Grant's camp. The two men of humble Midwestern origins understood one another and the terrible arithmetic of the Civil War.

Cold Harbor

Over the next 10 days, Grant made considerable progress. He kept moving to Lee's right flank, and Lee was, time and again, compelled to move his army south-by-southeast. Not only did this bring Lee away from the direct line to Richmond, but it increased the risk that Grant would corner Lee and bring about a thundering battle that would end the conflict once and for all.

By the beginning of June, Lee was ensconced in a strong defensive position at Cold Harbor, not far from the James River. Grant was, by nature, a cautious man, accustomed to feeling his way before making a move, but at Cold Harbor he sensed the opportunity for a crushing battle that would destroy Lee's Army of Northern Virginia. He could not have been more wrong.

Attacking on a broad front, across fields, against Confederates fighting over stone walls and earthen ramparts, Grant's Army of the Potomac suffered about 7,000 men killed, wounded, or missing in one hour. This was the single most terrible 60 minutes of the entire war, even worse than the famed

Pickett's Charge at Gettysburg the year before. Years later, in his memoirs, Grant wrote, "I have always regretted that the last assault at Cold Harbor was ever made."

Neither Grant nor Lee covered himself in glory in the days immediately following the battle. Grant asked Lee, by flag of truce, for permission to bury the Union dead, but Lee refused, for a variety of reasons. The result was that the screams of wounded and dying men kept living men, on both sides, awake through several nights.

If the calls for Grant's head that were issued by newspapermen had been loud before, they rose to an absolute clamor. *Fire him*, they wrote, time and again.

President Lincoln stood by Grant. And just two weeks after Cold Harbor, Grant vindicated the president's trust.

Richmond and Petersburg

Lee's entire army stood between Grant and Richmond, so late in June, Grant undertook one of the most daring actions of the Civil War. He had his army cross the James River, a mighty one by any standard, using pontoon bridges. Before Lee knew what was happening, Grant had brought 90,000 men across the James and into southern Virginia.

Rather than make straight for Richmond, though, Grant aimed at Petersburg, 20 miles to the south. This city was the central hub for all railroad lines—and therefore for all supplies and ammunition—for Richmond. Grant's leading units reached Petersburg just hours too late; a Confederate regiment got there first, ensuring there would be a siege of that town. But Grant was aiming at more than just Richmond: He proposed to envelop and eventually capture Lee's entire army.

By the beginning of July, the Army of Northern Virginia was strung out in camps between Richmond and Petersburg, and the Army of the Potomac was digging trenches and building fortifications that surrounded it. Neither Grant nor Lee was an ideal "siege" general—both preferred the quick strike, the

Grant was the first general to devise a coordinated strategy that would strike from multiple directions and the first to understand the concepts of total war. After Philip Sheridan and William T. Sherman followed Grant's strategies and Grant forced Lee to evacuate Richmond, Lee surrendered his army at Appomattox Court House. Pictured is Grant at his camp headquarters.

surprise maneuver. But the circumstances of the war conspired to bring them into what can only be called a "death grip," with both armies holding on for dear life.

Once the siege of Petersburg began, Grant turned to a group of engineers, asking them to find a way through the Confederate defenses. The group worked feverishly for three weeks, and on the morning of July 30, 1864, they exploded a set of devices that shook the ground, opening up a large crater underneath the outer Confederate defenses. As planned, Grant's Union troops charged in, taking the Confederates completely by surprise, but circumstances went against the offense.

The crater was so big and its indentations so vast that many Union troops charged forth only to become sitting ducks; Confederates rained down bullets upon the men milling about in the man-made crater. Nearly 4,000 Union men were killed or wounded or went missing on that terrible day.

By now, Grant had weathered so many battles and his men had suffered so many casualties that there were few calls for Lincoln to remove him from command. Grant settled in for what promised to be a very long siege, and President Lincoln continued to express every confidence in his general's performance.

Month after month, Grant and his men continued their inexorable envelopment of Richmond and Petersburg. By the beginning of 1865, the siege lines ran for nearly 200 miles, and it was difficult to keep track of all the men in the field.

Grant was greatly cheered by the continuing success of his second-in-command, William Tecumseh Sherman. In the autumn of 1864, Sherman captured Atlanta, and in the winter of 1864–1865 he drove on to the Atlantic coast, creating great devastation. His men fanned out in a 60-mile-wide column, tearing up railroad ties and wrecking farms and plantations. Southerners remember Sherman as the architect of their miseries, but everything that he did was sanctioned both by Grant and by President Lincoln.

For his part, Grant stayed within the siege lines and waited for what he knew must be the end of Confederate resistance. Late in March, President and Mrs. Lincoln came by ship to see the disposition of federal troops and to visit General and Mrs. Grant (Julia had joined Ulysses in the field). It was a rare occasion when anyone other than Grant mounted the war horse Cincinnati, but President Lincoln had the honor and pulled it off with style (Lincoln was a fine horseman).

GENERAL AND MRS. GRANT

In 1864, Congress lifted Grant to the highest rank seen since the time of George Washington. Grant was like George Washington in another way: both men had their wives with them in camp, whenever it was possible.

Grant even had brought his eldest son, Frederick, along on his early campaigns in Kentucky and Tennessee. Julia joined her husband as often as she could during the Western campaigns, but his victories in the East meant she could live with him most of the time at City Point, a Union camp near the Richmond-Petersburg lines.

Having Julia close at hand definitely lifted Grant's spirits; those who knew him best thought him at his cheeriest during the last months of the long siege. But there were complications, including one raised by a conflict between Mrs. Grant and Mrs. Lincoln.

The First Lady, a nervous, easily agitated person, came to dislike the general's wife, who exuded a rather pompous "know-it-all" attitude. On one occasion, the Lincolns and Grants discussed what might be done with Confederate president Jefferson Davis, when captured. The First Lady directed the question to Julia, who deftly turned it to what she claimed was Mr. Lincoln's good and generous nature. Mrs. Lincoln became angry with this, and she and Mrs. Grant became quiet adversaries.

It may have been on this occasion that Mrs. Grant offended Mrs. Lincoln, but whether it was here or two weeks later, there is no doubt that the latter took a firm dislike to the former, something that had important repercussions in the future. Grant and Lincoln were oblivious to their wives' clashing; they were intent on seeing the war prosecuted to its end.

President Lincoln gave Grant broad powers to negotiate the surrender of the Confederate enemy, but anything Grant did must be forwarded to Washington for Lincoln's approval. With that understanding, the president returned to Washington, and the general returned to the battle lines.

THE ROAD TO APPOMATTOX

On April 1, 1865, the starving remnants of the Army of Northern Virginia broke out of the siege of Richmond and Petersburg. Hungry, weary, and bereft of nearly all resources, the Virginians still managed to escape the siege and make a run to the west.

Grant's Army of the Potomac was after them in no time, and though the troops moved quickly, there was no doubt as to the final outcome. The last real battle of the Virginia campaign, fought at Sailor's Creek, was a complete Union victory; it was apparent that there was little fight remaining in the enemy.

When Lee and the Army of Northern Virginia reached Appomattox, they found Grant close behind them and General Philip Sheridan's column straight ahead. With no possible chance left, Lee sent his first communication to Grant on April 7 and met him at Appomattox Court House on the afternoon of April 9, as described in Chapter One.

GOOD FRIDAY

Lee surrendered to Grant on Sunday, April 9, which was Palm Sunday of the year 1865. Grant remained at Appomattox only a short time before returning to Washington, D.C., where, on Thursday and Friday of the following week, he met privately

During the Civil War, Lincoln continued to support Grant even when others called for Grant's removal. Immediately after Lee's surrender, Grant served as a pallbearer at President Lincoln's funeral. This drawing shows Grant at the tomb of Abraham Lincoln in Springfield, Illinois.

with President Lincoln. The president commended Grant for bringing the war in Virginia to a close, and he approved of the terms Grant had given Lee and the Army of Northern Virginia. The two Midwestern men seemed as in harmony as ever.

Their wives, on the other hand, were very much in conflict. First, there had been an unpleasant moment at City Point, outside the siege of Petersburg, and second, there had been another personal conflict in Washington, D.C. Julia Grant had come to dislike, perhaps even loathe, the First Lady. So, when President Lincoln asked General Grant if he and his wife would accompany him and Mrs. Lincoln to the theater on the night of Friday, April 14, Grant politely declined. He and Mrs. Grant had to leave the city that afternoon, he said, in order to visit two of their children in school in New Jersey. The president accepted Grant's answer with good humor, and the two men agreed to meet the following week. Lincoln would need Grant by his side in order to sort out the difficult matter of peace.

Leaving Washington, D.C., General and Mrs. Grant took the train north. They disembarked at Philadelphia for a change of cars, and there Grant received a telegram from the nation's capital: President Lincoln had been shot and killed.

The good will and harmony that prevailed on Palm Sunday—the day of Lee's surrender—were shattered by the violence of Good Friday.

The Highest Offices

Rushing from Philadelphia to Washington, General Grant arrived to find that the president was dead, the secretary of war had been wounded, and an attempt had been made on the vice president's life. This was a crisis of the highest magnitude.

JOHNSON SUCCEEDS

To a considerable degree, the U.S. government weathered the shock in good order. Vice President Andrew Johnson was quickly sworn in as the seventeenth president. Secretary of War Stanton recovered from his wounds. But one great loss was irreparable. Lincoln was dead.

As late as 1864, Lincoln had been considered a good leader but not a great one. But his Second Inaugural Address, delivered in March 1865, and his merciful attitude toward the defeated

South, had him poised to become the most popular, and perhaps the most successful, of all presidents. John Wilkes Booth's act of shooting Lincoln in Ford's Theatre turned Lincoln into a martyr, and Americans today still see him as he was in April 1865—a tall, solemn, and dignified man a bit shy of 60.

Lincoln's death thrust Grant into the spotlight. At Lincoln's funeral, Grant stood at the head of the line, head bowed, a spectacle of personal and political grief. Andrew Johnson was the new president, but Grant was the man Americans trusted most. The conqueror of Robert E. Lee and the magnanimous general at Appomattox had the nation's gratitude—he also carried its hopes.

Grant had no immediate desire for high political office. For the first time in his life, he was at a pinnacle from which it seemed nothing could dislodge him. Given the title of general of the armies (a permanent title with a $21,000 salary) by Congress, he basked in what seemed to be an unending series of triumphs. The people of Philadelphia gave him a splendid home, as did the people of Galena, Illinois. All talk of Grant the drunkard faded away; Grant seemed like the man of the hour.

Grant did not have a strong desire to enter politics, but politics came to him.

RECONSTRUCTION

The 12 years that followed President Lincoln's death are generally described as the period of Reconstruction, a difficult period in which Northern politicians and generals attempted to bind up the nation's wounds in order to bring North and South together. Still, there were innumerable obstacles.

President Andrew Johnson was a Southerner by birth, from Tennessee, but he had backed the Union from the beginning of the Civil War. Succeeding Lincoln in office was no small challenge for anyone, but it was especially difficult for Andrew Johnson, a man of limited education who possessed a stubborn mentality. While he had always been a Union man, Johnson did

Andrew Johnson succeeded Lincoln as president. His policies after Reconstruction, his hurry to re-incorporate the former Confederates back into the Union, and his vetoes of civil rights bills embroiled him in a bitter dispute with Republicans during a time when the human cost of the war led to demands for harsh policies. Late in Johnson's administration, Grant quarreled with the president and aligned himself with Radical Republicans.

not think black Americans were equal to white ones—not even close. While he delighted in having leading Confederate politicians come to ask him for clemency (which he usually gave), Johnson wished to see the Southern states restored to the Union in short order and without preconditions. If 5 million African

Americans had become "officially" free, they did not find much comfort or assistance from Johnson's administration.

Grant, whom everyone called simply "the General," was in a difficult position. In temperament and attitude, he was closer to Abraham Lincoln than to Andrew Johnson, but as general of the armies, he clearly owed his full allegiance to the new president. Then too, Grant had never been an ardent abolitionist. While he believed slavery was wrong, Grant had never joined abolitionist societies or made speeches on behalf of African Americans; to be fair, one can say that Lincoln also had been a lukewarm abolitionist, at least until 1863.

Grant also shared at least one thing with Johnson: both men wished to see the South restored to the Union with a minimum of humiliating conditions imposed upon the former. Grant had given generous terms to Lee at Appomattox Court House; those terms were now labeled the "spirit of Appomattox." Many Northerners wished to see the war over and done with, a thing of the past. Had there not been 5 million African Americans to consider, this might have been possible.

THE ELECTION OF 1868

In the spring of 1868, Grant learned that many leading members of the Republican Party, the party of Lincoln, intended to make him their presidential nominee for that year's election. Grant certainly was not averse to the idea of the highest office, and his wife was all for it, but he knew that it entailed risk. In 1868, he was at the height of his popularity, and he had built up a modest fortune through his general in chief's salary and from the gifts of many admirers. If he were elected, he would have an even larger salary ($25,000) but he would have to forego the safety of a salary for life; even more, he would have to spend a great deal on White House entertainment.

Whether Grant accepted the nomination from personal ambition or from a desire to be of service to the nation is difficult to say, but it is clear that he knew he was needed. The Republican

Party had nearly impeached President Johnson—the impeachment trial in the Senate failed by one vote—and it needed a new standard-bearer. Who better than the greatest Civil War general—perhaps even the greatest living general?

Grant sent a telegram to the nominating convention with a short acceptance speech that ended with the cryptic words "Let us have peace." Whether this meant an end to conflict between

FREEDOM

The news spread around Southern farms and plantations in 1863 and 1864. President Lincoln had officially freed all slaves living in the states then in rebellion.

Some blacks seized the moment and ran off from the farm or plantation where they lived. Some were caught and brought back, but many found their way to Union lines, where generals like Grant called them "contraband."

Other African Americans had to wait until the Confederacy's military might crumbled; in Virginia this meant the spring of 1865, while in far-off Texas it meant waiting until the summer of that year. But by the autumn of 1865, virtually all African Americans knew they were free, and the question was, how should they live?

Former slaves had skills, but they were shut out of occupations whenever possible. The slaves in some cities (New Orleans comes to mind) had more marketable skills and could make a living, but most had to return to a farm or plantation—and not necessarily the one from which they had come—to work as sharecroppers with former white masters.

North and South or between Republicans and Democrats was hard to say. The phrase caught on, and American voters began to identify Grant with "peace," much as they had previously thought him synonymous with "unconditional surrender."

Grant and the vice-presidential nominee, Schuyler Colfax, ran against a Democratic ticket of Horatio Seymour and Francis Blair Jr. Many observers believed the election would be a blow-

Sharecropping meant long, hard hours of work and little return at the end of the harvest, but it was the best most African Americans could do. There were some exceptions to the general rule, though, and a handful of black Americans did do well, financially and politically.

About 14 African Americans were elected to the U.S. House of Representatives in the 10 years following the war, and a large number of others held posts in state legislatures; there was even one black governor. Though African Americans were delighted to have members of their race advance in politics, there was a definite downside. White Southerners began to speak of "slave masters" and of blacks running the South. Like most propaganda, this idea had just enough truth—a kernel of it—to make many people believe that black Southerners oppressed white ones in the decade of Reconstruction.

The result was that, when federal troops were withdrawn in 1877, newly elected white legislators wrote the infamous "Black Codes," legislation that effectively blocked African Americans from high office and kept almost all blacks away from the polls. The noble idea of Reconstruction had yielded a poisonous crop, one that led to decades of "Jim Crow" legislation and restriction of blacks in Southern states.

Although Grant was a reluctant politician, he felt it was his duty to accept the presidential nomination in 1868. Grant had a tense relationship with President Johnson, which culminated in his support of Johnson's impeachment. At the time, Grant was very popular, having been promoted to a military rank that had not been held by any other American except George Washington.

out in Grant's favor, but by 1868 he had been identified with the policies of Reconstruction, something loathed by most white Southerners. Seymour and Blair knew where their advantage lay; they ran handbills and advertisements proclaiming that America was a "white man's country," hinting that something else would happen if Grant won. In the end, Grant and Colfax won by a narrow majority in the popular vote and by a large margin in the Electoral College. Though no one said it very loudly at the time, it became clear over time that African-American votes, especially in Southern states, had practically won Grant the election.

COMMANDER IN CHIEF

Grant had been many things in life: a tanner, a captain, a cutter of wood. He had progressed to become a colonel, a brigadier general, a major general, and finally general of all the armies. But on March 4, 1869, he went one step further, to the highest of all American posts: he became commander in chief.

He was not ready or right for the task.

It is a painful truth, one that most Americans are loathe to admit, but the American voter has often elected military men, some of whom were simply not right for the office. Zachary Taylor, Grant's old Mexican War commander, was one example. Elected president in 1848, he had died in office in 1850—fortunately, some said. Franklin Pierce, a comrade-in-arms from the Mexican War, had been elected in 1852; during four years in office, he had done little to nothing to prevent the increasing tension between North and South.

The talents that make a great military man often do not recombine to make a great chief executive. Certainly this was true in Grant's case.

FIRST TERM

Coming into office in March 1869, Grant was ambitious for one thing: to end the lingering animosity between North and South.

He cared about African Americans, but only in the abstract. He felt much more bonded to white Southerners, whom he admired as military men and over whom he despaired concerning common sense. If only white Southerners could see, Grant lamented, that their obstructionist ways hurt themselves and the entire country.

To his credit, Grant did what he could to protect African Americans. Military units were deployed on a number of occasions, and in 1871, the Justice Department was used to root out the Ku Klux Klan, a terrorist organization of bigots who wished to return blacks to slavery. But there seemed to be no end to the problems in the South, and as his first term wore on, Grant grew weary of the whole subject; to be fair, so did most Northerners of that time.

Grant showed initiative in international affairs. He continued pressure, which had begun during the Johnson administration, for an international body to decide the claims of U.S. citizens against the British government for assistance given to the Confederates during the war. This resulted in the landmark *Alabama* Claims of 1871, which established the precedent for international adjudication of such claims. Grant also sought to have the United States annex Santo Domingo (present-day Haiti) in order to make it part of the United States. His efforts ended when the Senate refused to ratify the treaty. But Grant's worst difficulties were domestic and financial. The boy who had offered $25 for the Ohio horse had not yet overcome his tendency to spend too much.

BLACK FRIDAY

Speculators and financial conmen found their way, however peripherally, into the Grant family. Abel Corbin, a financier in his late sixties, married Grant's younger sister Jennie. Assuring his two co-conspirators, Jay Gould and Jim Fisk, that he could persuade the president to follow his lead financially, Corbin set in motion the events that led to “Black Friday” on September 23, 1869.

The price of gold had hovered around $160 an ounce for some time, and Jay Gould and Jim Fisk wanted to drive it sharply upward in order to fuel a speculation boom on which they could cash out. Corbin had indeed used his familial connection with Grant to gain support, but when Grant learned that his new brother-in-law was in bed with the speculators, he turned against Corbin. Sending a letter of warning (written by Julia to Jennie), Grant readied the government for a major sale in gold.

Fisk, Gould, and Corbin failed to see the danger, and at about noon on Black Friday, Wall Street received the U.S. government’s order for the sale of $4 million in gold. The price of gold plummeted to about $130 per ounce, where it remained for some time. Dozens, if not hundreds, of speculators were ruined. Abel and Jennie Corbin gave up the Wall Street game and moved to New Jersey.

A congressional investigation followed, in which Julia’s letter to her sister-in-law was revealed. No direct link was ever established between the First Family and the financial scandal, but plenty of people believed—right or wrong—that Julia had been a major profiteer in the affair. It was a sad way to begin the Grant administration.

During the Civil War, Grant had shown a new style in his finances. Saving much of his salary, he had made good investments, including buying his father-in-law’s farm, White Haven, just outside of St. Louis. During his White House years, Grant spent a good deal of money turning White Haven into a horse-breeding farm. He knew horses better than almost anyone, and he made good selections, but the farm became a continual bleed on his personal finances. Much worse, he allowed his administration to become embroiled in large-scale financial speculation.

THE WHITE HOUSE

Grant's children were 19, 17, 14, and 10 when he moved into the White House in January 1869. His was the largest family seen there since that of Abraham Lincoln.

Grant's oldest son, Frederick, lived very much in his father's shadow; try as he might, he could not establish himself as an independent person. The second son, Ulysses, had an easier time finding his way and establishing his own identity. The third child and only daughter, Ellen, better known as Nellie, had a very mixed record. Her parents doted on her and her brothers adored her, but the admiration may have gone to her head, and in 1874 she married a British adventurer named Algernon Charles Frederick Sartoris. He had a magnificent long name but little else to recommend him. The only son of a low-level British bureaucrat, Sartoris became an expert at passing himself off as a member of the British aristocracy, something he assuredly was not. Visiting Washington, D.C., Sartoris met and courted Nellie, and he married her at the White House on May 22, 1874.

The wedding was the biggest social event seen at the president's mansion in decades, and virtually everyone in Washington wished to attend. As it turned out, Grant decided that invitations would be extended only to friends and relatives, so many politicians and their wives felt snubbed. The wedding was a magnificent affair, and President and Mrs. Grant accompanied the young couple to New York City to see them off on a ship headed to the British Isles.

The marriage was not a happy one. Sartoris was not so much a disappointment as a fraud, and the Grants later regretted having allowed their only daughter to leave the country.

Although Grant won re-election by a landslide, his second term was burdened by various scandals. Still, he was able to accomplish some good work, including enacting the Civil Rights Act of 1875, which gave equal rights to all people, and the passage of the Force Acts of 1870 and 1871, which took a hard line against the Ku Klux Klan. Here, Grant signs the Ku Klux Klan Force bill at the Capitol in 1871.

No one who knew Grant ever called him anything but honest: he was conscientious about debts and paid to the last penny. But as president, he showed a truly blind side toward the actions of others, including some members of his family.

SECOND TERM

There was little question Grant would be renominated by the Republican Party in 1872. Even though his first term had been undistinguished, he was, quite simply, the man most Republicans identified as their natural leader.

Grant won an easier election victory in 1872, defeating former newspaperman Horace Greeley in the general election. But there was no fundamental change in policy, no new direction for Grant or for the Republican Party.

The only solid accomplishment of Grant's second term was a clampdown on the activities of the Ku Klux Klan (KKK). Grant always had hoped that white Southerners would come to their senses and see that the federal government did more good than harm, but the actions of the KKK—mostly directed against African Americans—continued to increase. Grant authorized a Justice Department inquiry, and federal troops rounded up almost 1,000 KKK members in Southern states. Grant never received his due, either at the time or from historians since, for having broken the power of the KKK—the organization did not gain strength again until about 1920, though by then it was concerned with anti-immigrant and anti-Catholic feelings rather than only anti-black ones.

SCANDALS

Most historians who have examined Grant's record have come to the same conclusion about his presidential years. Grant, they tell us, was honest to the core, never making a penny out of his numerous contacts while president, but he had a terrible habit of loyalty. Time and again, he entrusted government affairs to men unworthy of the honor; and time and again, he stood behind them even when it was shown they had fleeced the government.

The Crédit Mobilier scandal, which involved the use of government funds from the building of the transcontinental railroad, broke in 1872, the year Grant ran for re-election. Not only his vice president, Schuyler Colfax, but also his new vice presidential nominee, Henry Wilson, were implicated. Grant stood by both men.

The Whiskey Ring scandal broke in 1874. Grant brought into his administration a man who searched diligently for the truth, but when it was revealed that Grant's secretary of the treasury, Orville Babcock, was among the profiteers, Grant allowed him to resign, thereby avoiding a painful trial in the Senate. One is forced to the painful conclusion that Grant, so fine a judge of men and horses on the battlefield, was a terrible judge when it came to men and money while he was in government service. His was the most scandal-plagued administration of the nineteenth century, and the number of men indicted in his eight years of office was not exceeded until the administration of Richard M. Nixon (1969–1974).

AN END TO POLITICS

Ulysses and Julia Grant left the White House in the spring of 1877. Grant was happy to be done with the office and with politics in general; he had been sorely tested during the previous eight years, and his health had suffered. Grant was 30 pounds heavier leaving the White House than entering it, and he was no longer as athletic as in the past. For her part, Julia Grant continued to think of the White House years as the best of their lives.

Circling the Globe

Jules Verne's popular novel *Around the World in Eighty Days* was published in French in 1873 and translated into English soon after. Thanks to the growth of railroads and an increase in the number of steamships—not to mention the assistance of the telegraph—it was becoming possible to circle the globe much faster than before. Record speed was not the object, however; travelers in the time of Ulysses Grant wished to take their time, to see the sights, and to record their impressions for posterity.

OVER THE ATLANTIC

Ulysses and Julia left the United States in the spring of 1877. The fact of their departure was well-known; less known was their itinerary, which would, to some extent, be made up as they went along. But they sailed, like so many other Americans of their time, in the direction of the rising sun, and they made their first landfall in Old England.

The Grants appeared in London that same spring, where they made quite a splash. First they met Albert, the Prince of Wales, and then his mother, Queen Victoria. Crossing the Channel to Belgium, the Grants met King Leopold, and they visited Cologne and Frankfurt before heading south to the Swiss Alps. So far there was no special hurry to their travel, but neither was there a distinguishable rhyme or reason to their movements. John Russell Young, the journalist who accompanied them, noted that wherever they went, the Grants were the center of attention, with the general receiving the lion's share. Kings, queens, and emperors showed great interest in the former president, but common folk, especially the British working class, were just as keen—they thought of Grant as the leader of the first "people's" army.

From Switzerland, the Grants doubled back, heading for England and then Scotland. There were ceremonial visits to Scottish castles and English coastal villages, as well as a special trip to see the birthplace of William Shakespeare. Grant received one of his most thunderous welcomes from the people of Tyneside, who seemed to view him as the man for a new generation. Thanking the people for their applause, Grant gave a typically short and nondramatic speech, in which he extolled the virtues of the working man. From there it was on to France.

THE CONTINENT

France was a republic in 1877, but the dreams of martial glory under Napoleon lived on. Grant did not identify with Napoleon in any way, shape, or form, but Mrs. Grant held a romantic view of the great military leader—perhaps thinking of him like her own husband. She was thrilled with Napoleon's tomb at Les Invalides. Grant himself preferred the Louvre, already the repository of many artistic treasures, and both he and Julia liked the splendid gardens of Paris. Typically, they did not stay in one place for long; soon they were on their way south to Italy.

The mountain of Vesuvius and the ruins of Pompeii already held a special attraction for many tourists, and the Grants were no exception to the rule. From there, the Grants went on to Naples, skipped to Gibraltar, then returned to Sicily to visit Palermo, Messina, and Mount Etna. Then it was off to Malta, the island of Capri, and on to Egypt, where they visited Alexandria and the Pyramids and took a boat down the Nile as far as Karnak. No Middle Eastern trip would be complete without seeing the Holy Land, so the Grants visited Jaffa, Nazareth, Bethlehem, and Jerusalem, where they went to the Wailing Wall (the oldest section of Jerusalem's walls, which dates back to the time of King Solomon).

Leaving the Holy Land, the Grants went to Constantinople (present-day Istanbul), then crossed to Greece, where they saw the Acropolis, and then on to Rome, Venice, Florence, and Milan. Traveling to northern Europe over land, the Grants saw Holland, Berlin, and Potsdam, where Grant discussed the Civil War with Otto von Bismarck, chancellor of the German Empire and a statesman who many people considered the equal of Abraham Lincoln: Both men were nation builders.

Grant's conversation with Bismarck ran to discussion of the Civil War.

"You are so happily placed," said Bismarck, "in America that you need fear no wars. What always seemed so sad to me about your last great war was that you were fighting your own people."

"But it had to be done," Grant replied.

"Yes," said Bismarck, "you had to save the Union, just as we had to save Germany."

"Not only [to] save the Union but [to] destroy slavery," was Grant's reply.

"I suppose, however, the Union was the real sentiment, the dominant sentiment," said Bismarck.

After the end of his second term, Grant and his wife spent two years traveling the world (1877–1879). Wherever they went there were huge crowds. Here is Grant (*seated, center*) with a group of tourists in Karnak, Egypt, in 1879.

"In the beginning, yes," said Grant, "but as soon as slavery fired upon the flag it was felt, we all felt, even those who did not object to slaves, that slavery must be destroyed. We felt that it was a stain to the Union that men should be bought and sold like cattle."

Leaving Germany, the Grants went to Denmark, Norway, and Sweden, visiting the Land of the Lapps along the way. From there it was on to St. Petersburg and Moscow, the two capitals of Czarist Russia, then westward to Poland and Austria.

Many people criticized the Grants' travel itinerary, for there seemed to be no overall plan; Ulysses and Julia simply went where and when it pleased them. There was a short tour of the wine country of southern France, followed by a visit to Spain and Portugal, followed by an even more incongruous visit to Ireland.

By now the Grants had pretty much played out their sightseeing of Europe.

TO THE ORIENT

In the late nineteenth century, "the Orient" meant almost anything east of the Suez Canal. Ulysses and Julia had long since decided that theirs should be a genuine world tour, so they did not restrict themselves to the palaces and theaters of Europe. In the winter of 1877, they sailed down the Suez Canal, headed for India.

The Suez Canal, built by French engineers a decade earlier, made for a splendid and easy trip to the Indian Ocean; once in that sea, the Grants were able to reach India with little difficulty. Here they experienced the greatest variety yet.

India, in 1879, was ruled by the British Empire, but it had lost nothing of the splendor of earlier times. There were magnificent monuments that dated back more than 1,000 years; there was the Taj Mahal—already fabled for its beauty—and there were elephant rides and tours of temples. The Grants explored British India with vigor. They met with conjurors, watched egg dances, and observed serpent charmers. Quite a few Americans had visited India prior to 1879, but none had had the fame of Ulysses Grant or the nimble pen of John Russell Young. The Grants visited the capital cities of Agra and Lucknow, saw the Ganges River, and on the whole, may have been the first prominent American couple to see so much of India.

Nor was that all: The Grants proceeded to Burma and then Siam.

SOUTHEAST ASIA

If India was noted for the diversity of its peoples and the splendor of its monuments, then Siam (Thailand today) was best known for the beauty of its buildings and the harmony of its society. The King of Siam, Chulalongkorn, was a confirmed pro-Western monarch; he wished to maintain the ancient traditions of his land while adopting many aspects of Western life. The Grants found him a grave and helpful host.

From there it was on to Hong Kong and then to mainland China. Here the Grants truly were on their own, for few Americans had come this way (though one who had slipped through was Frederick Townsend Ward, a military adventurer of the 1860s). The Grants saw the mountains of rice and tea in the harbor of Canton and then moved inland to the capital city of Peking (present-day Beijing).

Peking had been the capital of China for more than 300 years, and it boasted the fabulous Forbidden City, which was the residence of the emperor, his wives and concubines, and the eunuchs who ran the imperial bureaucracy. The Grants met the emperor and his mother (who was the real power behind the throne); they made little comment on Chinese traditions, but

CONVERSATIONS WITH GRANT

John Russell Young, a gifted writer, was adept at describing the scenes in India, China, and elsewhere, but there are times in reading his two-volume work when it seems as if he and Grant were oblivious to the rest of the world. Many an evening was spent on deck, discussing not the price of tea in China or the customs of Japan, but rather the way in which Grant and Lee had maneuvered before Richmond or the role of West Pointers like Thomas "Stonewall" Jackson.

Grant was not a vain man, but the accumulated glory of his Civil War years contrasted sharply with the painful letdown of his White House ones, so he spent evening after evening describing specific Civil War situations. Yes, he said, many Union generals were slow to realize that the grand objective was Lee's army, rather than Richmond or any other capital. No, he said, General Pemberton could not have held Vicksburg a single day longer than he did.

John Russell Young wrote at length of the tradition of foot-binding, then prevalent in upper-class Chinese families. His description may have been among the first that many Americans had of this ancient practice.

The Grants saw the Great Wall of China, first built in the time of the fierce First Emperor (around 200 B.C.) and then rebuilt in the times of the Ming dynasty of the fourteenth and fifteenth centuries. Grant made no comment about the military use or applicability of the Great Wall; he seems to have saved his choice comments for European observers such as Bismarck. But Grant's tongue was loosened when the traveling Americans sailed across the narrow sea and reached Japan.

Grant was simply enchanted by Japan. Everything and everyone, he said, was neat and orderly. Everyone seemed to understand his or her place in Japanese society; doubtless, this appealed to Grant's military mind. But he reveled in the charm and beauty of Japanese life, ranging from the exquisite flower gardens to the stone temples. Here, he said, was an example of what humans could accomplish on Earth.

Grant met the emperor of Japan in Nikko. The meeting itself was not so unusual, until the emperor came forward to shake Grant's hand. When asked about a precedent, Japanese courtiers simply could not remember a time when this had happened before.

HEADED HOME

The Grants left Japan in an American sailing ship in September 1878. It took them 18 days to reach the Sandwich Islands (present-day Hawaii), where they delighted in the charm and simplicity of island life. From there it was another 10 days before they saw the Golden Gate (the gap between San Francisco and Marin County). Sailing into the City by the Bay, the Grants were nearly overwhelmed by congratulations and applause. Grant never wrote of his reception in San Francisco, but it cannot have escaped his mind that this had been the scene of one of his greatest humiliations—back in 1854, he had resigned from the army

After a year and a half abroad, Grant was homesick. He decided to return home through Asia. Grant befriended Viceroy Li Hung-chang (*right*) in Tientsin, China, and wrote that he was "probably the most intelligent and most advanced ruler—if not man—in China." At Peking he was asked to settle a dispute with Japan over the Ryukyu Islands.

and headed home from this very spot. Now, 25 years later, he came as the conquering hero, one of the first prominent Americans ever to circle the globe.

ONE MORE TIME

In the summer of 1880, the Republican Party sent its delegates to a convention in Chicago. Grant did not enter his name in the lists, but many of his friends thought he should run one more time. A halfhearted effort was made to introduce Grant's name at the convention—he won some delegates—but it was doomed to failure. Whether Grant actually would have accepted the opportunity to run for a third time is not known. He had become heartily sick of politics, even if Julia Grant missed the White House days.

One Last Campaign

Grant's homecoming in 1879 was not the beginning of a "happily ever after" story. The man who had braved homesickness, depression, alcoholism, and the slight of his neighbors, had one more campaign to wage—and it would be the hardest of his life.

FINANCES

To Americans then, and to many people today, it seems incredible that a man of such stature and of such gift in military matters should have become penniless, but it is all too true. Grant had never been a good manager of money, and his judgment of character—so often superb in military matters—was poor when it came to financial concerns.

Returning in 1879, Grant had a choice of where to settle down. The citizens of Philadelphia had given him a fine home back in 1865, though he had sold it, and the people of New York City, as well as those of Galena, Illinois, were eager to do the same. Grant eventually accepted the generosity of New Yorkers, and he made the Empire State his home.

Grant had made plenty of money over the past 15 years, but he had spent most of it. Much had gone to a failed endeavor—trying to make Julia's childhood estate of White Haven into a horse-breeding farm. Grant was an excellent judge of horses, but he was a poor one of the expenses required, and eventually he had to sell the estate just to break even. If Grant had kept his rank of general of the armies (the one granted by Congress in 1865), he would have had a pension for life, but this was forfeited upon becoming president in 1869. Remarkable as it seems, there simply was no pension for former presidents, and Grant was very much on his own financially.

Even so, Grant might have been able to get along, in a reduced fashion, were it not for his wife and children. Julia had many virtues but modesty and the ability to live below her means were not among them. She reminded Grant, time and again, that he was a great man and that the family should live in a fine style. By this point in life, Grant agreed with his wife, and they undertook some risky investments to better their financial condition.

Early in May 1884, Grant went to the home of William Vanderbilt to ask for a $100,000 loan to bolster the sagging conditions of the firm of Grant and Ward (Grant's son was a principal in the business). Vanderbilt cheerfully agreed, asking for no collateral, but the Grant fortunes collapsed the next day when Grant and Ward went into bankruptcy. The financier Ward went to prison for 10 years; Grant and his son were not charged with any crime, but they had lost everything.

So bad was it that Grant began selling swords and mementos from his Civil War years. His private library of 5,000 volumes was sold off, and yet it still appeared the Grants would live in disgraceful poverty for the rest of their lives. Grant had endured low and painful times in the past, but this outstretched them all.

WRITING

Just before the collapse of the financial firm, Grant had been commissioned to write two Civil War articles for *The Century Magazine*. The writing was good, crisp, and to the point, and Grant earned a few dollars on the side. The real surprise was what came next.

Mark Twain, already America's most famous humorist, read *The Century* articles and decided that Grant had a fine writing style. More, Twain had long admired Grant from afar, calling him one of the great men of the time. So, in the autumn of 1884, Twain called on Grant and asked if they might collaborate on his memoirs.

No record exists of their conversation, but one imagines that Grant was surprised to hear the greatest writer of the time asking to collaborate with him. Twain also proposed that he publish the memoirs himself, removing the need for a traditional publisher. This would enable Twain to pay a much higher royalty rate for the books, perhaps as much as 40 percent of each book sold. Naturally, Grant was pleased to hear this, as he and his family were in desperate straits.

THE DOCTOR'S NOTICE

At around the same time that he entered into an agreement with Twain, Grant experienced a series of physical disturbances. There were pains in his hands, his arms, and his throat, all of a type he had never experienced before. A doctor was summoned, and the news was quick and painful: Grant had cancer of the throat.

General Grant Worked on His Memoirs Even When Fatal Illness Overtook Him.

In 1885, at the time that Grant was writing his memoirs, he was bankrupt and suffering from throat cancer. Mark Twain offered Grant a generous contract, and Grant finished the book just a few days before his death. Today, the two-volume set is considered one of the finest memoirs ever written.

It was too late for any type of operation; the cancer had spread. Grant had to accept that his days on Earth truly were numbered.

Grant took the news with the same stoic fatalism he had shown in war, in peace, in prosperity, and in poverty. There was nothing to be done about the cancer, but he did have an opportunity to redress his financial woes.

Grant had already begun writing his memoirs; now he went to them with a will. By the spring of 1885, the Grant family was living on an estate called Mount McGregor, a few miles outside of Saratoga Springs, New York. Doctors came and went, as did orderlies, but Grant's main business was gritting his teeth through the pain while scratching away with pencil and pen:

> My family is American, and has been for generations, in all its branches, direct and collateral.

These opening words of *Personal Memoirs* seek to emphasize his middle-American roots; he was a son of the soil, one born and bred to life in the Early Republic.

> A military life had no charms for me, and I had not the faintest idea of staying in the army even if I should be graduated [from West Point].

This statement, in the second chapter, was one of the most surprising to Grant's readers. They did not know, as we do today, that his father had practically forced him to go to West Point or that Grant had been a rather aimless young man. To his thousands, perhaps millions, of admirers, Grant seemed like the very embodiment of Yankee stoicism.

> We were sent to provoke a fight, but it was essential that Mexico should commence it.

Forty years had passed since Grant's Mexican War experience, but he had not changed his mind about the conflict; to him, it seemed that the U.S. government had deliberately goaded Mexico into a fight that culminated in American possession of much of the Southwest.

> Now, the right of revolution is an inherent one.

Here, in Chapter 16, Grant seemed to support the South's inherent right to rebel against the North. But he went on to explain his belief that the framers of the Constitution had been wise to provide means for the amendment of that document, and that the Southern rebels of 1861 would have done better to lay their grievances on the table, rather than to take up arms against the federal government.

> I have always regretted that the last assault at Cold Harbor was ever made.

This was Grant's sole concession to his military critics, to those who claimed he was a "butcher" who threw men into battle and to their deaths.

> Our armies were composed of men who were able to read, men who knew what they were fighting for, and could not be induced to serve as soldiers, except in an emergency when the safety of the nation was involved.

Here, in Chapter 70, Grant made a deliberate comparison between American soldiers of the Civil War and European soldiers of the Crimean War and the Franco-Prussian War. European soldiers were brave, he wrote, but they usually did not understand the causes for which they fought. American fighters, Grant claimed, were better-educated and more able to make choices for themselves. While not everyone would agree with his conclusion, it has since been used in many instances to explain the difference between American soldiers and their counterparts from other parts of the world.

Grant's next-to-last paragraph reiterated a famous statement from his election campaign of 1868:

> I believe we are on the eve of a new era, when there is to be great harmony between the [former] Federal and the [former] Confederate. I cannot stay to be a living witness to the correctness of this prophecy, but I feel within me that it is to be so. . . . Let us have peace.

Grant finished the writing on July 19, 1885. His last campaign was a successful one.

Grant died at Mount McGregor on July 25, 1885. His last words, as quoted by friends and reported in the *New York Times*, were, "I hope that nobody will be distressed on my account."

EULOGIES

Sadness prevailed throughout the nation. Very few Southerners rejoiced to hear of their former conqueror's death; on the contrary, many made public their admiration of the man. The great majority of Northerners expressed sadness that the Civil War victor, the embodiment of a generation of soldiers, was gone.

Grant's body was brought to New York City and laid to rest a week after his death. Several Confederate generals, including his old friend (and foe) Simon Bolivar Buckner, were among the pallbearers.

A subscription was taken up for the creation of a fine tomb, and in 1897, Grant's remains, followed by those of his beloved Julia in 1902, were laid to rest in the impressive "Grant's Tomb." There, on a quiet section of the Hudson just above Columbia University and the hubbub of the metropolis, they remain.

THE ROYALTIES

Grant's *Personal Memoirs* was published in December 1885 by Mark Twain. Sales of the two-volume masterpiece were simply

General Grant National Mausoleum, also called Grant's Tomb, is the largest mausoleum in North America. It is modeled on a modern variation of the tomb of Mausolus at Halicarnassus, one of the seven wonders of the world.

sensational. It was a rare Union veteran that did not wish to purchase the great general's memoirs, to read about Vicksburg, Donelson, and The Wilderness. So many copies were sold that the family's 40 percent royalty eventually came to over $400,000, allowing Julia (who survived Ulysses by 17 years) and the family to live in comfort.

As important as the money was, the quality of the writing became even more so. Grant's memoirs were widely read and admired in the decade following his death, and critics over the next century would heap praise upon them, calling them the best set of military memoirs written since the time of Julius Caesar.

THE LEGACY

At the time of his death, Grant was one of the most beloved of Americans, but not necessarily one of the most admired ones. Men and women still thrilled to hear of his Civil War victories, but his lackluster two terms as president had dulled his legacy. Things became worse over the next two generations.

By the 1930s, presidential historians were convinced that Grant was among the very worst of American presidents—almost, but not quite, at the bottom. Warren G. Harding, president from 1921 to 1923, usually beat Grant out for the lowest rank.

By the late 1970s, many historians had decided that Richard M. Nixon, the only man ever to resign from the presidency, was the worst president in the nation's history. This lifted Grant, and Warren G. Harding, a little higher on the list.

There has been no major reassessment of Grant's presidency since the 1980s. Most scholars continue to believe he was among the least effectual of all American chief executives. But Grant the man and Grant the soldier has made a strong comeback.

Beginning in 1990—the year that Ken Burns's documentary *The Civil War* played on public television stations—there has been an increased interest both in the war and in the generation of young men that fought on either side. Those who study the Civil War often come away with an even greater appreciation for Grant the man, one who battled depression, drink, and financial woes. Those who are keen on the Civil War battles usually emerge with great respect for the man who freed the "Father of Waters" from the South and who defeated Robert E. Lee.

In the second chapter we saw that Grant's middle name, which later became his first name, was given to him by an aunt who had read the recent translation of *Telemachus*, the story of Ulysses's son. It took Ulysses of Greek fame 20 years to make it home after the Trojan War, and then he had to do battle with the evil suitors who wanted his wife's hand and his estate. It took Ulysses of American fame only four years of Civil War generalship to make his name and fortune, but it took all the rest of his years even to approach the lofty summit he had reached with Lee's surrender at Appomattox.

Grant's is a truly American story, complete with tales of small-town life and big-city ambitions, but it also has classical themes: those of father-son relations, of war and peace, and, finally, those of failure and redemption.

CHRONOLOGY

1821 Jesse Root Grant marries Hannah Simpson.

1822 Hiram Ulysses Grant born in Ohio.

1823 Grant family moves from Point Pleasant to Georgetown.

1826 Julia Boggs Dent born in Missouri.

1839 Hiram Ulysses Grant goes to West Point where he becomes, on paper, Ulysses S. Grant.

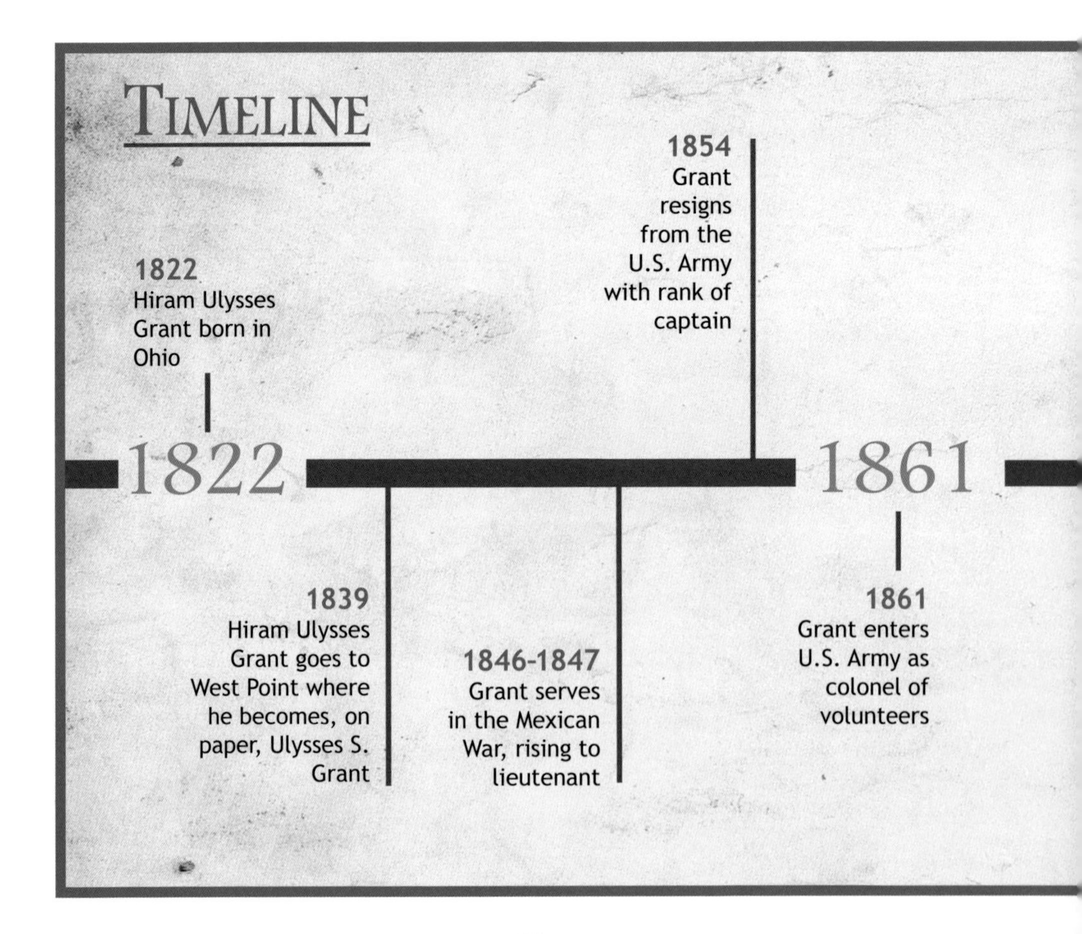

1843	Grant graduates from West Point, is commissioned a second lieutenant.
1845	Grant summoned to active duty in Louisiana and then Texas.
1846-1847	Grant serves in the Mexican War, rising to lieutenant.
1848	Grant marries Julia Boggs Dent.
1848-1852	The Grants move to Detroit, then to the West Coast.
1852	4th U.S. Regiment ordered to the West Coast.
1854	Grant resigns from the U.S. Army with rank of captain.

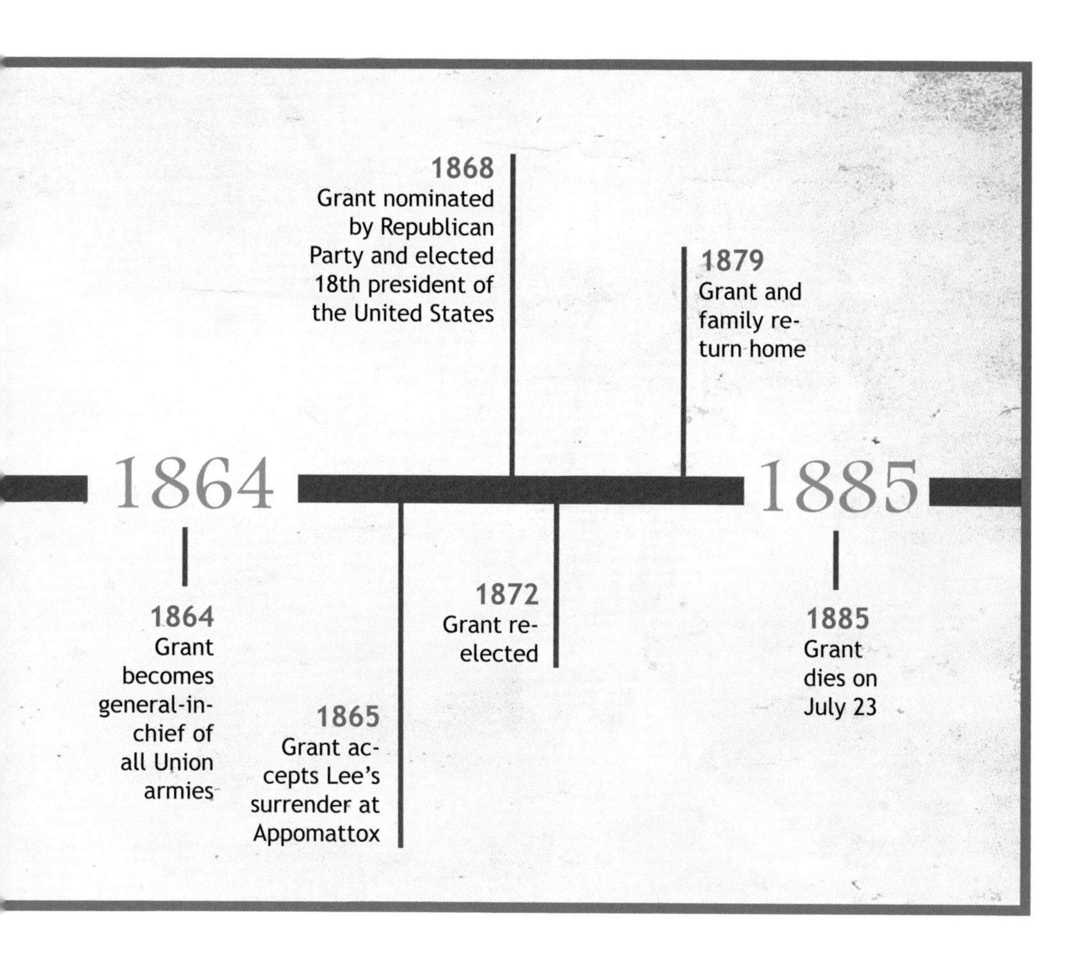

1860 Grant goes to work in his father's tanning shop in Galena, Illinois.

1861 Grant enters U.S. Army as colonel of volunteers.

1862 Grant captures Forts Henry and Donelson, fights Battle of Shiloh.

1863 Grant captures Fort Vicksburg on Mississippi River.

1864 Grant becomes general in chief of all Union armies.

Grant fights Lee at The Wilderness, Spotsylvania Court House, and Cold Harbor.

1865 The siege of Richmond ends with Union victory.

Grant accepts Lee's surrender at Appomattox.

1866 Grant becomes General of the Army of the United States and a member of the presidential cabinet.

1868 Grant splits with President Andrew Johnson.

Grant nominated by Republican Party and elected eighteenth president of the United States.

1869 Grant inaugurated.

Black Friday financial scandal.

1872 Grant re-elected.

1873 Jesse Grant dies.

Whiskey Ring Scandal.

1877 Grant leaves office, departs for worldwide tour.

1879 Grant and family return home.

1884 Grant impoverished by collapse of Grant and Ward.

Grant and Mark Twain agree to work on his memoirs.

1885 Grant finishes his writing on July 19.

Grant dies on July 23.

Grant buried in Riverside Park.

1902 Julia Grant dies and is interred with Ulysses in Grant's Tomb.

GLOSSARY

Army of Northern Virginia The 70,000-man army led by Robert E. Lee and, until his death in 1863, Stonewall Jackson. The army was renowned for its ability to move fast and strike hard, frequently catching its opponent, the Army of the Potomac, off guard.

Army of Occupation Name given to the 6,000-man American army stationed on the northern side of the Rio Grande in 1846. Lieutenant Grant was one of its members.

Army of the Potomac The 110,000-man army centered on Washington, D.C., and the Potomac River. Developed and refined by General George B. McClellan, it became the instrument of victory under the leadership of Ulysses S. Grant.

Border States Four states—Maryland, Delaware, Kentucky, and Missouri—that were neither pro-Union nor definitely Confederate when the Civil War began.

Confederate States of America The 11 states that joined together after leaving the Union in the winter of 1860–1861.

Deep Southern States A band, or belt, of states, commencing with South Carolina and stretching all the way to Texas. Compare with Upper Southern States.

Dragoons Cavalrymen.

Father of Waters The Mississippi River. The title comes from a Native American name.

General of the Armies A title held by George Washington and then by Ulysses S. Grant. A special elevation of general's rank.

Isthmus (of Panama) There was no Panama Canal until 1912. Until that time, people who wished to avoid the 9,000-mile journey around South America crossed the Isthmus at Panama or Nicaragua.

KKK The Ku Klux Klan, an organization formed by Confederate veterans soon after their defeat in the Civil War.

Lone Star Republic The original name for Texas. Given this title because, between 1836 and 1845, Texas was an independent nation.

Occident(al) All lands and water to the west of the Suez Canal.

Orient(al) All lands and waters to the east of the Suez Canal. Compare to Occident(al).

Reconstruction The attempt to reunite and reconstruct the nation in the 12 years following the Civil War.

Speculators Those who profit by buying and selling rapidly on Wall Street. Grant's first administration was plagued by reference to scandals of speculation.

Stars and Bars The flag of the Confederacy.

Stars and Stripes The flag of the Union.

Teetotaling Non-alcoholic.

Telemachus The Greek son of Ulysses, who waited for 20 years to see his father. Ulysses S. Grant received his name from relatives who were then reading the novel *Telemachus*.

Ulysses The Greek hero who took 20 years to return home after fighting in the Trojan War. His heroism is chronicled in *The Odyssey*.

Upper Southern States A band, or belt, of states, commencing with Virginia and stretching to Tennessee.

War Between the States The most common name for what we now call the Civil War.

Wilderness (The) A heavily wooded area just south of the Rappahannock River where Union and Confederate armies fought a series of terrible battles.

BIBLIOGRAPHY

Davis, Major General George B., et al. *The Official Military Atlas of the Civil War*. New York: Barnes and Noble Publishing, 2003.

Grant, Ulysses S. *Personal Memoirs of Ulysses S. Grant*. New York: Library of America, 1990.

Hunt, Frazier, and Robert Hunt. *Horses and Heroes: The Story of the Horse in America for 450 Years*. New York: Charles Scribner's Sons, 1949.

Korda, Michael. *Ulysses S. Grant: The Unlikely Hero*. New York: HarperCollins, 2004.

Lewis, Lloyd. *Captain Sam Grant*. Boston: Little, Brown and Company, 1950.

Longacre, Edward G. *General Ulysses S. Grant: The Soldier and the Man*. Cambridge, Mass.: Da Capo Press, 2006.

McFeely, William S. *Grant: A Biography*. New York: W.W. Norton & Co., 1981.

Meredith, Ray. *Mr. Lincoln's General: U.S. Grant*. New York:E.P. Dutton, 1959.

Perret, Geoffrey. *Ulysses S. Grant: Soldier & President*. New York: Random House, 1997.

Simon, John Y., ed. *Personal Memoirs of Julia Dent Grant*. New York: G.P. Putnam's Sons, 1975.

Simpson, Brooks D. *Let Us Have Peace: Ulysses S. Grant and the Politics of War & Reconstruction, 1861–1868*. Chapel Hill, N.C.: University of North Carolina Press, 1991.

Strong, Phil. *Horses and Americans*. Garden City, N.Y.: Garden City Publishing, 1939.

United States Military Academy. *Register of Graduates and Former Cadets of the United States Military Academy West Point: Bicentennial Edition* (2000).

Young, John Russell. *Around the World with General Grant: A Narrative of the Visit of General U.S. Grant, Ex-President of the United States*. New York: The American News Company, 1879.

FURTHER RESOURCES

Grant, Ulysses S. *Personal Memoirs of Ulysses S. Grant*. New York: Library of America, 1990.

Korda, Michael. *Ulysses S. Grant: The Unlikely Hero*. New York: HarperCollins, 2004.

Lewis, Lloyd. *Captain Sam Grant*. Boston: Little, Brown and Company, 1950.

WEB SITES

The Grant Monument Association: Grant's Tomb
http://grantstomb.org/ind-gma.html

National Park Service: Ulysses S. Grant—Slavery at White Haven
http://www.nps.gov/ulsg/historyculture/slaveryatwh.htm

The Ohio Historical Society: Grant Birthplace
http://ohsweb.ohiohistory.org/places/sw08/index.shtml

Ulysses S. Grant Homepage: Grant on Slavery
http://www.granthomepage.com/grantslavery.htm

Ulysses S. Grant Information Center: Ulysses S. Grant and his Horses
http://faculty.css.edu/mkelsey/usgrant/hors2.html

Vicksburg Campaign Trail
http://www.nps.gov/archive/vick/camptrail/sites/Louisiana-sites/HardTimesLA.htm

PICTURE CREDITS

PAGE

10: The Bridgeman Art Library
15: Courtesy of the Library of Congress, [00917r]
19: The Granger Collection
23: AP Images
27: Courtesy of the Library of Congress, [3g06126r]
32: Getty Images
36: Courtesy of the Library of Congress, [USZ62-101537]
40: Courtesy of the Library of Congress, [3c10714r]
43: Courtesy of the Library of Congress, [3b52027r]
49: The Bridgeman Art Library
51: Courtesy of the Library of Congress, [3g01910r]
55: Courtesy of the Library of Congress, [06457r]
61: AP Images
67: Courtesy of the Library of Congress, [01859r]
70: Courtesy of the Library of Congress, [04407r]
74: Courtesy of the Library of Congress, [3b50281r]
78: Courtesy of the Library of Congress, [00112r]
82: Courtesy of the Library of Congress, [3b48118r]
87: North Wind Picture Archive
93: Courtesy of the Library of Congress, [LC USZ62-92457]
97: © Corbis
101: Getty Images
105: AP Images

INDEX

ABOUT THE AUTHOR

Author **SAMUEL WILLARD CROMPTON** grew up playing Avalon Hill war games such as "Gettysburg" and "D-Day." A part-time professor of history at Westfield State College and Holyoke Community College, he is also a noted author, with over 40 titles to his credit. Crompton has written about Grant and Lee in *100 Military Leaders Who Shaped World History* and has appeared on the Military Channel's *First Command* program. An avid hiker and occasional bicyclist, he lives in the scenic Berkshire Hills of western Massachusetts.